Goff-Nelson Memorial Library
Tupper Lake, NY 12986

D0856035

FRONTIER JUSTICE

Book Two:
Martha

FRONTIER JUSTICE

Book Two: Martha

•

DON HEPLER

AVALON BOOKS
THOMAS BOUREGY AND COMPANY, INC.
401 LAFAYETTE STREET
NEW YORK, NEW YORK 10003

© Copyright 1995 by Don Hepler
Library of Congress Catalog Card Number: 95-094892
ISBN 0-8034-9150-6
All rights reserved.
All the characters in this book are fictitious,
and any resemblance to actual persons,
living or dead, is purely coincidental.

PRINTED IN THE UNITED STATES OF AMERICA
ON ACID-FREE PAPER
BY HADDON CRAFTSMEN, SCRANTON, PENNSYLVANIA

52,801
11/95

Goff-Nelson Memorial Library
Tupper Lake, NY 12986

FRONTIER JUSTICE

Book Two:
Martha

Chapter One

Cyrus Borlan was the twisted-up sheriff of
Brown Bear Creek. He didn't get the job because
he was good with a gun or even because he had
been a lawman before. He got the job because he
had been thrown from his horse and an old longhorn range bull had like to stomped him to death.

When the healing was finally done, he came out
of it with a half twist in the middle. To the left.
His right leg had also healed shorter than his left
by two inches or so. Anytime a body would see
him limping by all twisted up, stepping up and
down on his short leg, they'd think the wind was
blowing almighty hard outside.

Since Brown Bear Creek was a small town with
mostly good people, they took pity on Cyrus and

1

elected him sheriff. He was the first sheriff they ever had. They hadn't needed one before and frankly, they didn't need one now. It was a good thing, because Cyrus was not much of a sheriff even though he took the job seriously.

He'd get up with the sun because that's when everybody in Brown Bear Creek got up. He'd put on his hat, pull on his boots, and strap on that old cracked leather holster on the wide black belt. He'd check the loads in his model 1851 Navy Colt and stuff the big gun into his holster. Morning ablutions thus completed, he would go out and patrol the short boardwalks, one on each side of the main street, looking for bad men or crime or who knows what.

Rain or shine, that's where you'd find Cyrus. He'd stomp up one side, stutter-stepping on the wooden walk in a way that, once heard, was never forgotten. He'd cross over at the far end, which wasn't very far at all, and limp his way back. That was how he saw his job, and having been a cowboy and a hard worker, that was how he did it. That was also why he was the first to see them.

Front Street ran east and west, and when he looked south, past McGuffrey's Saloon, he could see two riders coming over the rolling bluff. They were still too far away to determine their identity, but Cyrus stopped and watched them ride slowly toward town. There was something familiar about the front rider, but he couldn't put his finger on it yet.

They weren't coming real fast, so he stumped on down to the end of the boardwalk, carefully avoiding that one board in front of Leman's Gun Shop that was weakened by the knot. He carefully one-stepped down the step at the end of the boardwalk and looked south once more. The two riders rode up on him.

"Mornin' Cyrus," said the front rider.

"Morning, Mr. Leech," said Cyrus. He peered at them without being too obvious. Wouldn't do to offend Mr. Leech, him being a landowner and all. Right off, Cyrus picked up on the bandage around Leech's leg.

"Run into some trouble?" Cyrus asked. Leech grinned tightly.

"Little bit," he said, then: "Indians." He had Cyrus's full attention.

"Around here?" he wanted to know.

"A week back," Leech explained, and Cyrus relaxed some. He looked over the other rider, then looked back again, forgetting not to be obvious. It *was* a woman, and dressed in man's clothes, too. Martha could see the surprise on his face and she smiled down at him.

"Hello," she said. He touched the brim of his hat.

"Howdy, ma'am," he said. He wanted to ask,

but that was something a man did not do out here, so he held his peace.

"Things been quiet around here?" Stacy asked.

Cyrus took off his hat and scratched at his matted hair like it was terrible difficult to remember what all had been going on.

"Pretty quiet," he said. "Lemuel got drunk a week past, and tried to knock out Robert's mule, but aside from that, nothing much." He watched the woman smile at that. She was a pretty thing under all those bulky clothes. He smiled back.

"Mules ought to stay away from drunks," Stacy observed as he kicked his horse into motion once more.

"That's the way I figured too," Cyrus said to their backs as they rode down Front Street and headed out toward the rising sun. Probably headed for Leech's ranch, Cyrus figured. Man's been away from home a few weeks, he's usually pretty anxious to set foot on his own land again. He stumped across the dry, dusty street and started his trek back along the boardwalk. Four more riders were just coming into town from the east. Going to be a busy day, looked like. He made sure his badge was showing plain, then stumped on down the boardwalk toward the strangers.

"Cyrus was just like you described him," Martha said. They were riding side by side. Stacy smiled over at her. He still couldn't believe that this wonderful, lovely woman had picked him. Good things like that normally didn't happen to him and it was going to take some getting used to.

"You didn't believe me, huh?" he asked.

"Seemed a little unlikely," she admitted. "He doesn't strike me as the sheriff type."

"Don't let his form fool you," Stacy said. "There's a whole manful of courage in that crooked little package. Would have been easy for him to let go and die lots of times, only he didn't. He got better. Folks around here look highly on courage. That's why they made him sheriff. He takes the job real serious."

"Don't take my meaning wrong," she said. "I like him. He reminds me of a little banty rooster that has been through a lot, but stays full of feisty just the same." Stacy grinned over at her. Lord how he liked to look at her!

"Full of feisty, huh. I like that. Not sure *he* would, though."

"He will like me," she said with a certainty. Stacy watched her riding beside him.

"I reckon he will," he said. They rode in silence for a while.

"How much longer until we are home?" Martha asked.

" 'Nother half day," he said. "We'll have supper tonight in our own house.'' She grinned over at him and shook her head gaily.

"My, that still sounds strange,'' she said.

"Any stranger than being called Mrs. Leech?'' he wanted to know.

"Nope,'' she admitted. "That was pretty strange too.'' They were referring to the first time that tall, skinny preacher had called her that . . . right after he had married them.

"You'd better get used to it,'' he said. "I think you would have a passel of trouble trying to get rid of me now.'' She rode closer, reached out, and patted him on the leg.

"Don't want to get rid of you,'' she said softly. He grinned like a schoolboy.

It was well into the afternoon when they topped a hill and Martha first saw her new home.

It was sitting in a little valley, maybe half a mile across. A stream meandered across the length of the valley. There were a couple dozen horses wandering loose around the valley, some standing in the stream drinking, others feeding on the scruffy grass. The house, a single-story affair little more than a big cabin with a front porch, sat almost dead center. Only a few steps to the side was the barn, a structure not any larger than the house itself. The impression was one of a lot of sky, a few animals, and a couple of lonely buildings in the middle of nowhere. Martha turned to Stacy and beamed.

"I love it," she said. Stacy looked at her, relieved.

"Like I said, it's not much," he said. "But it will be." He paused and she could tell that what he was about to say was very important to him. "It's ours now," he said. "Yours and mine." He hesitated as he searched for the words he wanted. Martha waited patiently, thinking about his words. It was theirs. All of his work in the past years he was now sharing with her. She, who had never really had anything in her young life, was now a ranch owner.

"Ranching is a gift to nobody," he went on. "It is a hard life, a demanding life, but together we can build something out here. We can make something you can see and get down and feel with your hands."

She had never heard him speak like that before, and realized she was hearing a man tell of his secret innermost dream. He was explaining it to her because it was important to him that she understand what was driving him; what was making him do the things he did. She held up her hand to stop him.

"You don't have to apologize to me," she said. "You don't have to explain it to me. I see what is down there, and I see what will be down there. We have been joined, and the two of us have been turned into just one of us together." Somehow, saying solemn, important things made her uncomfortable.

He thought about that for a moment, then grinned at her and winked.

"I hope you remember that when we have our first fight," he said. Martha laughed and they rode down the hill to her new home.

Stacy opened the door and stepped aside.

"Welcome home, Martha," he said. She smiled a little nervously and went in.

The place was a little bigger than it had looked from outside. There was a central room with wooden chairs and a fireplace. A small desk sat in the corner. The floor was bare wood, but clean. Two front windows looked out over the porch, and there were heavy wooden shutters on the inside of each that could be closed against the weather. They had small firing slots in them in case what they were closed against was worse than the weather.

"Kitchen's through there," he nodded at the open doorway leading toward the back of the house. Martha walked through the door and gave a little bleat of fear. There was a big, bearlike man standing in the kitchen looking at her with his mouth open. It was hard to say who was more surprised, but he got in his introductions first.

"Who are you?" he asked rather unpleasantly. Martha stepped back a step, then remembered that this was *her* kitchen now.

"Who are *you?*" she countered. Stacy stepped forward and held up his hands.

"Easy, you two," he said. "Martha, this is Lemuel and he sort of goes with the place. Lemuel, this is Martha. She sort of goes with the place too, since she is my wife." Lemuel couldn't have looked more surprised if somebody had hit him in the back of the head with a shovel.

"Your wife?" he said, amazed. "Your wife?" He studied Martha for a moment. She endured his hard gaze. He turned to Stacy.

"This a permanent thing?" he asked. Stacy grinned, but Martha was actually a little bit shocked at the impertinence of the question.

"She's my wife, my real wife, you idiot," he said. Lemuel turned his hard gaze on Martha again and looked her up and down. Then he turned away as if dismissing her.

"You folks can get out of my kitchen now," he said bluntly over his shoulder. "I'll put some more potatoes in the pot for dinner."

Martha felt her face flush as blood rushed to her head. She held her temper in check for the moment and looked to her husband for guidance. Stacy just grinned down at her and led the way from the kitchen. Martha followed, willing to bite back her anger until she found the lay of the land in her new home.

"You forgot to tell me about Lemuel," she said. He shrugged.

"He's been with me from the first," Stacy said. "Kind of like a permanent fixture around here." He turned away, then tossed back over his shoulder, more as an afterthought, "Good man in a fight."

"Not if you're a mule," Martha replied and heard her husband laugh. He opened the closed door that led from the main room to the bedroom and stepped aside. His expression was a little strange, like a naughty schoolboy. Gosh, he was embarrassed.

"This is the bedroom," he said without looking her in the eye. She walked in.

There was a double bed pushed up against the wall, a small table for a lamp between it and the corner. No headboard, though, and no quilt either, just a cheap rough blanket. The only window allowed the afternoon light to stream in. There was a single wooden chair in the corner and a small table with a pitcher and basin in the other corner. That was it.

She went over and felt the softness of the bed, then looked at Stacy with a wicked little grin. He blushed immediately and practically ran back into the front room. Martha smiled broadly and followed.

They went out on the front porch and looked out over the land. Their land.

"How far does it go?" she asked.

"Not real big," he said. " 'Least not yet. Few miles toward town and maybe twenty miles farther the other ways. Least that's how far the beeves are spread out." He looked out, remembering the hard work. "Mostly the cattle were wild," he said. "Although I did buy a couple from Phil Kelly, our neighbor."

"Neighbor?" she asked as she looked out at the wandering horses.

" 'Bout thirty miles south," he replied. "Married too, so you'll have a woman around to tell all your husband troubles to."

Martha sat down in one of the two wooden chairs.

"We have any money?" she asked.

"Not much," he admitted.

"I need some decent clothes."

"We can ride in tomorrow and pick up what you need," he said immediately. "Probably some things you might want to get for the house too."

"Probably," she said.

Stacy pulled the other chair over by hers and sat down opposite her, face serious.

"Look," he said. "It'll be all right. I know the place isn't much, but . . ."

She held up her hand and stopped him.

"Listen," she said. "I'm tired of you apologizing for our home. This is our *home*," she repeated, "our home." She hesitated as she searched for the right words. "You took a naked piece of land and started building this ranch from nothing. You should be proud of this place. I am." She waved her hand around. "Now there are two of us, and we can get twice as much done as before." She shook her finger at him in mock anger. "Don't ever let me hear you put our home down again, Mr. Leech. Not ever again."

He grinned over at her.

"Yes ma'am," he said. "Never again." She patted his knee and stood up.

"Now," she said, "I have one more thing I have to take care of before supper." And she went back in the house.

Lemuel was putting the peeled potatoes into a pot of boiling water.

"Lemuel," Martha said, "you are truly a horse's behind." He turned, shocked.

"What?" he asked.

"I said you are truly a horse's behind," she repeated loud and clear. "This is not your kitchen, this is *my* kitchen. If you *ever* try to boss me around in my own home again, I will take a belt to you. Do you understand?" Lemuel straightened to his full height and looked down on the woman. His great size made her look even smaller. He obviously didn't have any idea how to respond to her. She shook her finger in his face.

"Don't you tangle with me, mister," she said.

"You may have led a rough, tough life, but you haven't seen bad yet until you make me angry." She glared up at him, head tilted back so she could look him in the eye.

Lemuel looked down on her, expressionless for a long moment, then his hard face cracked and he smiled all over.

"I believe you, ma'am," he said, humor in his voice. "I truly do. Last thing in the world I want would be you beating on me with a belt." He waved his hand around. "Welcome home, Martha Leech," he said. "You want I should get out of your kitchen?"

"I want you should show me what you're doing about getting supper ready," she said. "You have any biscuits started?"

Out on the porch, Stacy listened to the two of them.

"You call those things biscuits?" he heard Martha say. "I've seen cannonballs smaller than that."

Lemuel sputtered for a moment, then said, "Biscuits got to be filling. I am cooking for working men out here, not some lady's tea party."

"Oh, well," Martha said. "We'll go ahead and cook them. Maybe we can use them to pound in fence posts."

"My biscuits will be light and fluffy," Lemuel said flatly.

"Compared to rocks, maybe," said Martha. In spite of his pretended offense, Lemuel laughed.

"You are sure a good talker," he said. "I ain't seen your biscuits yet."

"What smells in the oven?" Martha asked.

"That's a apple pie," Lemuel replied, a little proudly. Stacy heard the oven door open, then close.

"You call that a pie crust?" he heard Martha say.

"Oh, for cripes sake," from Lemuel.

Stacy grinned broadly, then got to his feet and stepped off the porch to tend to the horses. Looked like life was going to be all right around here.

52,801

Goff-Nelson Memorial Library
Tupper Lake, NY 12986

Chapter Two

Wesley Hader rested his small telescope on a rock and peered down over the valley floor checking his back trail. He steadied the glass with a view of the top of the hill across the valley and waited. The distant figure of a man on horseback soon broke the horizon followed by three others. He sighed.

"Buckled down on catching me, aren't you?" he mumbled to nobody in particular. The telescope snapped together and he slid backward until he was out of sight from the pursuers before he got to his feet and brushed himself off. His horse was standing there ground-tied, and she snorted softly.

"Looks like they're 'bout four hours behind us,

15

girl,'' Wesley said. Being alone so much, he had developed the habit of talking to his horse or even inanimate objects. Kind of peculiar how much he talked when he was alone because he almost never talked when there was someone to listen. He figured that someday somebody would catch him talking to a tree or something and have him locked up. Probably serve him right too.

Distant thunder mumbled off to the west and he studied the sky.

"Maybe rain in a couple 'a hours," he explained to the horse named Penny. "I figure we'll just rest up here a mite, then once it starts raining we'll hightail it north. Rain should cover our tracks if we're lucky."

He loosened the saddle some and the horse went back to tearing up mouthfuls of the sparse grass. Not a lot of nourishment in that sparse growth. He'd like to get her some grain pretty soon. Wesley took down his bedroll and laid it out on the ground. He planted his lanky form on top of it, covered his eyes with his hat, and was asleep in moments.

Just under two hours later, the first big drop splatted onto his hat, jarring him awake. He got up, stretched, then rolled the bed and tied it behind his saddle. Penny grunted when he tightened the cinch, and he swung aboard.

"Okay, girl," he said. "Off to the west for a

while, then when it's raining nice and hard, we'll swing north and run a bit.'' He booted her gently in the ribs and away they went toward the darkening horizon, leaving a straight line of tracks behind pointing due west.

In half an hour it was raining to beat the band, great sheets of water pushed by the gusty wind, blowing directly at them. Wesley neck-reined to the right and they headed north, rain pelting them from the side. Behind, the wind whipped the long grasses, blowing away any signs of their passing. Pounding rain flooded their tracks, and in less than ten minutes there was no sign they had ever existed.

Six days later Wesley finally came on a road, swung west and followed it toward the town that must be at the other end. He was bone weary. Too many days of steady riding. Too many days of going short on sleep. Too many days of just plain tired.

It wasn't much of a town that met his view when they topped a small rise—one street with a few buildings on either side and a couple of small homes scattered about where the storekeepers and their families led out their lives. Penny's hooves thumped small clouds of dust from the road as they rode in. Likely he could get her some oats here. He reached forward and patted the tired horse.

A twisted-up man with a shiny star on his chest met them at the edge of the boardwalk. Wesley reined in.

"Howdy," he said. He'd never seen a twisted-up sheriff before, but he had learned never to underestimate any man who had the brass to put on a badge.

"Howdy," from the sheriff.

"Lookin' for a place to put up my horse and then a place to get a bite," Wesley said.

"Livery at the end of the street," said the sheriff, nodding his head in that direction. He liked the way the man was going to take care of his horse first. Once a cowboy, always a cowboy. "You'll see the Railroad Cafe on the right as you ride through. Food is fair and you get plenty of it."

Wesley touched his hat. "Obliged," he said and booted Penny into motion once more. They clopped their way through the small town and Wesley could feel the sheriff's eyes on his back the whole way.

There was a small building with a corral at the end of the street. The big sign said LIVERY on the front. Wesley swung down. It felt real good not to be sitting on a horse for a change. He led Penny into the dim barn where a young boy was watching him.

"Howdy," said Wesley. The boy nodded solemnly. "She needs rubbing down and some grain."

"Costs fifty cents overnight and grain's a extra two bits," said the boy importantly. Wesley smiled. Nice to see a serious kid.

"Price is fine," he said. The boy looked at him up and down, then decided.

"In advance," he said. Wesley laughed out loud. He reckoned he didn't look so well-to-do after so long on the trail. He fished out a silver dollar from his meager supply and handed it to the boy.

"Probably just one night," he said. The boy nodded and took the reins. Wesley pulled his rifle from the boot and untied his saddlebags and bedroll. The boy led Penny back into the barn and tied her to a post. He disappeared for a moment and then came back and solemnly handed Wesley his quarter change.

"Any rooms in the hotel?" Wesley asked.

"Most likely," said the boy.

"Best steak in town?" from Wesley.

"Railroad Cafe," came the answer. "Only steak in town."

Wesley nodded; on an impulse he flipped the quarter to the boy.

"Take good care of the horse," he said. The boy's eyes widened with pleased surprise.

"Sure thing, mister," he came back. "Thanks a lot."

Wesley turned and walked out, cussing at himself for giving away a whole quarter when he had so few of them. A quarter was a lot of money, especially to a kid. He'd probably eat himself sick on penny candy or something, and someday Wesley would be eating snake on account of he didn't have that quarter for real food. A nickel would have been enough. A dime would have been more than generous. He sighed. Oh, well, what's done is done.

The hotel was right next to the livery. He stepped up on the boardwalk and went through the doors. A plain-looking woman was watching him from behind the desk.

"Howdy," she said, friendly-like. She had a nice smile.

"Howdy," and he smiled back. "Need a room overnight."

"One dollar and you don't have to share it neither, least not 'less we get real busy all of a sudden." He pondered on it, then nodded.

"Seems fair enough," he said. It was a lot of money, but it would be worth it to have a room and a real bed all to himself. Might as well go broke in style.

The room was better than he had any right to expect this far west. The bed was soft, although a little on the short side, and even bragged a headboard, obviously handmade. There was a small table with a basin and pitcher, and a window looking west along the backs of the other buildings on the street.

"How many rooms you have?" he asked.

"Five," she said with no small amount of pride evident in her voice.

"They all as nice as this?"

"Some better," she replied, obviously pleased that he was impressed. She waited a moment to see if he had more to say, then left and went back to the front. Wesley stood his rifle in the corner, dropped the saddlebags on the floor, and headed out for the restaurant, following the grumbling of his stomach.

The Railroad Cafe was next door, and not real large. It boasted three tables, all well used. There was not another customer in the place, but then it was pretty early in the day—six o'clock by the grandfather clock in the hotel lobby. He selected a spot away from the door with his back to the wall, and sat down. He could smell coffee. He had been out of coffee for four days and the smell was almost powerful enough to drink. A head poked out from the kitchen door.

It was a pretty head, he had to admit, young with brown eyes and crowned with brown hair tied up in a bun. She had a straight nose and a wide mouth, a feature he had always found attractive in women. Her eyebrows went up in surprise at the sight of a stranger.

"Howdy," she said and came out, wiping her hands on her apron. "What can I do for you?"

"Howdy, ma'am," he said. Wesley couldn't remember how long it had been since he talked to such a fine-looking woman. "Like some of that coffee and a steak if you have one."

"Sure do," she said brightly. "Cost you a dollar with all the fixin's including apple pie." Her smile was infectious, and he smiled right back.

"Bring 'er on," he said, and was a little sorry when she headed back into the kitchen and he was once more alone. She came back right away with a cup and the coffeepot, and when she set the cup down and poured it full, he could easily smell her faint perfume.

"You can work on that while I get your steak to cooking," she said. "You need more coffee just holler. Name's Alice, and I'll come a'running." She was not wearing any wedding ring. Likely it was her folk's cafe and she worked here. He wanted to ask her, but didn't.

"Thank you kindly," he said. He wanted to talk with her more, but had no idea what to say. He nestled the hot cup in his hands and sipped. It was wonderful. A man really missed coffee when he didn't have any. No matter how he made it, chicory just wasn't the same as real coffee.

The woman went back into the kitchen and Wesley sipped at the coffee, savoring every drop.

He watched three men ride up to the front, their forms made wavy by the plate glass window. They looked like cowboys, laughing and talking together as they tied up and came inside. They stopped short for a moment when they saw him, then appeared to ignore him as they went and sat at the far table. The oldest was maybe twenty. The Railroad Cafe was small and there was no way he could *not* hear every word they said.

"Poor old Ritchie has been all quivery for the last two weeks just thinking about comin' in here again," one of them jibed. The one named Ritchie, little more than a boy, looked embarrassed.

"Aww," he said. "You fellows don't know what you are talking about." Alice came out of the kitchen and walked over to their table. Ritchie's face turned beet red and his eyes never once rose from the floor. Wesley tried not to smile as he sipped at his coffee and pretended not to pay any attention to them.

"Hello, boys," she said. "What'll it be?" The other two snickered a little and Ritchie truly looked miserable.

"I'll have a steak with all the trimmings," said one. "Been too long eating Frank's cooking . . . or should I say burning."

"Ain't nothin' wrong with my cookin'," said the other. "Seems to me the problem's with the eater." Then to Alice: "I'll have the same, pretty lady.'' He nodded at Ritchie with his head. ''I think my friend here would just settle for having you hold his hand for a spell.''

Ritchie glared at the speaker, Frank, then spoke in a hushed voice.

''Don't pay them no mind, ma'am. Their folks didn't teach them no manners a'tall.'' He glanced up at her, then looked down again. ''I'll have a steak too, ma'am,'' he said. He couldn't be more than sixteen years old, Wesley figured. He was wearing a man's clothes though, probably doing a man's work, and his gun was clean.

''Comin' up,'' she said. She appeared not to notice the side play going on. She brought them coffee and also filled Wesley's cup again, then disappeared into the kitchen once more. The three cowboys watched her disappear through the door.

''She is right good-lookin','' said Frank. ''You do have a good eye for the ladies for one so young,'' he added. Ritchie glared at him and the other spoke to him.

''I don't recollect hearin' you say too much to her,'' he observed. ''Seems like when we were on the trail I kept hearing you tell about all the lovely things you was going to say to her.'' Ritchie smiled sheepishly.

''We ought to hire her to go along with us,'' said Frank. ''This is the first time he has shut up in over a week.''

"You are right," said the other. "Thought I was going to have to shoot him for a while there, just to get some peace and quiet." They sipped at their coffee and fell into a companionable silence. "Howdy, boys," said Wesley. They looked at him and howdied right back.

"You boys know where a man can get work around here?" he asked. They studied him for a while.

"You might try out at the Circle L," said Frank. "Boss said he was lookin' for a couple more good hands."

"That is just what I have got," Wesley observed. Frank grinned.

"This is your lucky day, then," Frank said. "Boss and his wife are in town for supplies. We come in with them. They will be in here shortly for supper. I'll point him out."

"Obliged," said Wesley. Frank studied him for a little longer, obviously wanting to know more about the man who might be working alongside him, but asking questions like that was just not done. Not polite. Not safe either, sometimes.

Alice brought out Wesley's steak on a platter. It was the same size as the platter with one end covered with home-fried potatoes.

"Looks good," Wesley said as she set it in front of him.

"Hope you like it," said Alice. "That'll be one dollar, please."

Wesley dug a silver dollar from his pocket and handed it to her. He placed it in her hand, feeling the softness of her palm against his fingertips. Been a long time since he had been so close to a woman.

"Thanks a lot," she said.

"Thank you," said Wesley. He took knife and fork to hand and dug in. It was good. He was about half finished when she brought out the cowboys' food, and he was just sopping up the last of the juice from his plate with a chunk of bread when the door opened.

A man and a woman came in. The man's gaze swept the room, stopping for a moment on Wesley. He studied the stranger for a moment, then swung his gaze to the cowboys, and a grin cracked his face.

"Howdy, Boss," said Frank around a mouthful of steak.

Wesley had time to study the two newcomers as they sat down at the only available table. The man sat on the side facing the door, a trait that Wes noticed and appreciated. He had a Colt strapped to his side and the air of a man who knew how to use it. The woman was dressed in a plain go-to-town gingham dress and her hair was pinned up. Alice came out from the back.

"Hello, Mr. Leech," she said, then, "Hi, Martha." The woman smiled back and it was like the whole room lit up.

"Hello, Alice," she said, and her tone left no doubt she was glad to see her.

"Can I feed you today?" Alice asked.

"Sure can," the woman said. "Okay if I come back and talk while you're working?"

"You come on ahead," Alice said. "It's been over a month since I last saw you." The woman—Martha, Alice had called her—got to her feet and the two disappeared into the back. Wesley sipped at his coffee and cleared his throat. Mr. Leech looked over.

"Howdy," said Wesley. Leech nodded. "Name's Wesley Hader and I'm looking for an honest job," Wes went on. Leech studied him.

The stranger was tall and slim, with a face that showed signs of a life spent in the open. He was hard to age, maybe twenty-five, maybe a little older. His gun was clean and his hands were hard. He looked Leech right in the eye as he was being appraised, and Stacy liked that in a man. He was dressed like a cowhand down to his spurs, and his clothes were old enough so he wasn't a tenderfoot.

"Pay's thirty a month," said Leech. The man nodded.

"Obliged," he said. Stacy indicated the other table with a nod of his head.

"These three desperadoes are Frank, Ritchie, and William. They work for the Circle L too." Wesley looked at the others.

"We have met in a manner of speaking," he said. Martha came out from the kitchen with a cup of coffee for her husband.

"This is my wife, Martha," Leech went on. "Martha, this is Wesley Hader, a new hand." Wesley rose to his feet.

"Howdy, ma'am," he said. His eyes dropped to the floor, then he caught himself and brought them back up to her face. A man didn't drop his eyes to anybody, not if he was a real man. Her gaze was open and direct and he could sense a little curiosity behind her look.

"Hello, Mr. Hader," she said. "Welcome to the Circle L."

"My name is Leech," the man went on. "Stacy Leech. That's where the L came from in Circle L," he added. Wes extended his hand and the two shook hands. It was done. He was hired.

"We'll be riding out after supper," Leech went on. "You need a horse?"

"Got one," Wes said.

"You can keep him or sell him," Leech said. "Long as you work for me you can ride my horses."

"Reckon I'll keep her," Wes said. "I already paid for a room for tonight," he added. "Be okay if I show up tomorrow?"

"Tomorrow's fine," Leech said and turned to his steak. Martha sat down and did the same.

"C'mon over here and set if you've a mind to," said Frank. Wesley wasn't wild about the idea of sitting with his back to the door, but it wouldn't be polite to ignore the men he was about to work with.

"Obliged," he said and took his coffee over to their table. He could feel the woman's eyes on him as he walked across the room.

"Name's Frank Able," said the man, extending his hand. "This here's Ritchie McGowen, and that sorry excuse for a man is William Boone, no relation to Daniel." Wes shook hands all around. Their hands were rough as his, the hands of working cowhands.

Alice brought over his apple pie, still warm from the oven.

"Here you are, mister," she said. "It would seem you have fallen in with bad companions." Wes smiled up at her.

"I will see to their souls, ma'am," he said. He didn't know why he said that. It just came to him. And that was how he got the handle Preacher.

Chapter Three

Yellow Knife sat astride his horse and watched the line of his people as they moved north. He was a full warrior now, even more, he was the leader of warriors. His fight with the white men had made him well respected. His taking of prisoners and trading them for the rifle that now rested on his lap was noted by the elders and brought him a reputation for wisdom. His voice was listened to in the council.

Best of all; most wondrous of all the rewards, was Twisted Hair. His eye picked her out walking with the other women. She appeared not to be looking at him, but he could tell she was watching him. He could feel the weight of her eyes, and he loved her. It still didn't seem possible that she truly belonged to him now, but he had offered two of the white men's horses and her father had accepted, and now she shared his tipi and his life.

Her cooking was not yet so great, but when she held him in the night, the taste of her food did not seem to matter so much. Besides, she would learn just as her mother had, just as all other Sioux women had, from the beginning of time.

He kicked his horse into motion and rode along the line, passing Twisted Hair slowly. He pretended to pay her no mind, but his heart felt light to be near her again, and for an instant their eyes met. She smiled and he smiled before he remembered that he was a warrior and kicked his horse into a canter, leaving her behind.

Chief Stone Hand watched all this with tolerant amusement, although his face gave no clues as to his thoughts. Yellow Knife was not yet certain enough of himself as a husband or a man to openly show his feelings toward his new wife, but Stone Hand could remember his own first wife, and could understand.

Yellow Knife had gone from youth to man in short order, and many of the others who once ignored and tolerated him as just another child now looked up to him and respected his judgment.

Stone Hand felt the burning in his chest and tried to ignore it as he watched the young warrior, but he could not ignore it for long. The pain demanded his attention, and he coughed that awful cough, feeling like his chest was tearing up inside. He did not let his face show any of the terrible pain that went with the cough, but when he wiped his lips there was a trace of blood on his fingers. He forced the pain away from his mind and studied Yellow Knife as he rode along.

The young man now had the respect of the people. He had shown good judgment with trading. He had shown bravery in battle with the White Eyes. If only he was not so young. Stone Hand felt the pain growing in his chest once more and a sudden cough ripped from his lips before he could control it. From the line of walking women he saw his wife looking at him. Her face was expressionless, but he knew what she was thinking. He nodded slightly to the woman he would soon leave behind and turned his attention back to Yellow Knife. He wiped his lips without noticing the blood this time, for his concentration was on the one biggest decision a chief must ever make.

His eye took in the beauty of the rolling hills and waving grass; the ragged line as his people moved along in their unhurried pace. So many years he had seen them move such. So many years he had led them. Now he was tired and he could not breathe; it was time for the reins to pass to someone younger and healthier.

He coughed again, long wracking coughs that

left his lips red, his chest afire, and his body gasping for air when there was plenty of air all around him. He felt his wife looking at his back, but he ignored the feeling. In spite of the pain, in spite of the gasping, he felt good in his heart. He had made the decision, now it only remained to tell his people.

As his breath came back he once more took in the beauty of the land that he loved so well. It was sad that he would soon leave this place. It was also fitting that he do so. There was a time for all things to live and a time for all things to move aside and move on. His life had been a good one.

His way of dying was hard and hurt plenty, but he would die well because his father and grandfather were watching from the other side. Soon he would join them, but first he would make them proud. In his mind he thanked them for the hard way of dying, for now he could truly show them he was worthy.

The wonder of his people and the rolling hills swept over him and he submerged himself in them until another bout of coughing tore him back to the here and now.

The day's march was finished, the women had cooked, and all had eaten. Chief Stone Hand took his pipe and lit it, being careful not to let any of the smoke get down into his lungs, for it would not do for him to fall into a fit of coughing. His council of warriors and old men watched him carefully. Stone Hand passed the pipe and they smoked in silence for a while. When the pipe returned to him, he carefully set it on the robe beside him and looked at the group of men, some of whom had been his advisers from the very first day he was chief; others were new to the council. He cleared his throat.

"I have thought on this long and hard," he said. "I will burden my people no longer. I shall not go on when you break camp tomorrow." There was no sign of surprise from the assembled men, and he had expected none.

"I am going to name your new chief and he shall be chief from the moment I utter his name. I am certain I am correct in this choice, and there will be no discussion about it." Their faces did not change, but Stone Hand knew that several of the mens' hearts were beating fast. Several of them were ambitious, and ambition was not altogether a bad thing. He was sorry that he would have to disappoint them, but he knew his decision was the correct one.

"Your new chief," he said simply and without ceremony, "is Yellow Knife." Now the signs of surprise were clearly visible on some faces. Especially on the face of the new chief named Yellow Knife. He leaped to his feet.

"What?" he asked. Stone Hand held out the pipe to him.

"Take the pipe, Chief," he said. Yellow Knife hesitated, then came forward and took the pipe the same way he would have grasped a live rattlesnake. Stone Hand nodded. It was done.

"The rest of you will leave us now," he said. The men of the council, some young, some old, rose and left, each man nodding slightly to Yellow Knife as they departed. He stood there holding the pipe, stunned to the very core of his being. Then they were alone.

"Sit, Yellow Knife," said Stone Hand, and Yellow Knife dropped to the robe across from the old chief. No. That man was no longer chief. Now he was just an old man, an old dying man.

All of his life this old man had been his leader and Yellow Knife never questioned any of his decisions, but now Yellow Knife was certain the old man had just made a big mistake. Perhaps Stone Hand's sick chest had caused him to say something he did not mean. He wanted to question the old man, wanted to explain that he was not ready to be chief, did not want to be chief, had never even considered being chief. Manners won out, and he sat in silence and waited for the old man to speak.

"There is a confederation of the Sioux and Cheyenne by the river the Little Bighorn. Many warriors will be there and I am sorry I shall miss it.'' Although Yellow Knife looked across at him silently, Stone Hand could still see the surprise deep in his eyes. He almost smiled, but the pain in his chest reminded him and he did not.

"This will be an important thing," he went on. "More important than the treaty meeting ten winters ago." He wanted to cough, but fought down the urge.

"At that meeting Chief Bear Rib spoke the words for us all and I can remember his words as if they were but spoken yesterday. Take heed, for these are the words and feelings that have governed me as I led, and I hope they will govern you now that it is your turn to lead." Yellow Knife made as if to speak, but fell silent when Stone Hand raised his hand.

" 'To whom does this land belong?' Bear Rib asked. 'I believe it belongs to me. If you ask me for a piece of land I will not give it. I cannot spare it, and I like it very much. All this country on either side of the river belongs to me . . . and if you, my brother, should ask me for it, I would not give it to you, for I like it and I hope you will listen to me.' '' Stone Hand leaned back and tried to catch his breath once more. It would not hurt to give Yellow Knife a moment to think on those words. He was pleased to see how serious the young man was taking his words.

"I am afraid the Whites did not listen well," he finally said. "I think they are trying to take our land from us." He sighed and looked away.

"I think there may be nothing we can do to stop them," he said softly, "For they are as many as the grains of wheat and we cannot kill them all."

"We will fight!" Yellow Knife said defiantly.

Stone Hand looked at him and remembered what it was like to be a warrior.

"You are young to be a chief," he said. "You must remember that the young are wont to think with their feelings and not with their heart. Because you are now the leader of all the people, young and old alike, their welfare must come before all. Think with your heart and look over your feelings."

"We cannot give up our land," said Yellow Knife.

"No," Stone Hand said sadly. "You must fight. But know this. You cannot win in the end." Yellow Knife looked puzzled.

"Pick your battles carefully," Stone Hand suggested. "Do not choose to fight unless you can win. Some of your warriors will die and it will tear at you, but that is a burden of being chief and you cannot help this. You will wear the burden of young men dying like all of us before you, and you will make your decisions based on what is in your heart and that is all."

Yellow Knife watched the old man gasp for breath once more. Much was swimming around in his head.

"Now go," said the old man. "I am weary." Yellow Knife rose and looked down on this old man whom he loved.

"I thank you, Stone Hand," he said. He was just leaving the tipi when he heard the old man's faint words.

"Don't be too sure," he said.

The morning dawned blood red and beautiful, but Yellow Knife knew that such a morning sometimes promised storms later in the day. All the tipis were down save one, and the people, his people now, moved out in their northward journey. He sat astride his horse and watched them as they filed past.

There was something different, some subtle change in them all. He was now the chief, and he knew that his life would never be the same. Stone Hand's wife walked past with her sister, and she did not look at him as she went by but he could feel the change in her too.

He turned his horse and looked back. The lone tipi sat there like a forgotten landmark. The old man stood in front, trying to stand straight and tall, but slightly bent from the pain of his chest. Across the distance the two men looked at one another, then Yellow Knife turned his horse to the north and did not look back again.

The name of Stone Hand would be spoken no more, for it was disrespectful to speak of the dead.

Chapter Four

Martha looked through the wavy glass over the sink, enjoying the clear morning light. Her man, Stacy, was walking across to the corral. Even after these four months she still found it strange to think of him as her man; it still seemed strange to be married. What a change for a woman to suddenly share the life of a man, to know him, really know him. His inner thoughts and dreams were there for her to see, only she had never imagined that men could be so deep and yet so simple, almost single-minded in their constant striving toward their goal.

Stacy wanted to be a respectable rancher, and that was pretty much all there was to him. Oh, he sometimes had other ideas; sometimes had moments of wildness and animal-like behavior, but on the whole he was trying hard to be civilized and make a safe and secure home for the two of them—and their children should they have any.

Stacy watched as Wesley finished breaking a horse, then called him over and talked to him for a minute. Wesley nodded and Stacy headed back toward the house. He saw her looking from the window and grinned a boyish grin and gave a little wave. He loved her, loved sharing himself and his life with her, and made it plain that he did. Martha loved him too, more than she had ever loved anyone or anything in this life. It was her greatest joy to surprise him with something thoughtful and pleasant; maybe something'as simple as a glass of lemonade in the heat of the day. He was always so grateful, and it amazed her and pleased her that she could take care of her man just as well as any other woman. She listened to him come through the front door, heard the familiar sound as he walked back to the kitchen.

"Hi, babe," he said. She liked the nickname. Of course he only used it when they were alone.

"Hi yourself," she said back. "Glass of water?" she offered.

"No, thanks." He sat down at the scruffy table, fingers absently feeling the roughness of some of the scratches. She kept it clean though, cleaner than it had ever been most likely. "Got word that

the Railroad Cafe wants a couple more beeves.
Restaurant business must be pretty good. Anyhow,
I told Wes to cut out a couple and drive them to
town. Figured you might want to go along and see
Alice. Woman needs to have another woman to
talk to once in a while.''

"You coming too?" she asked. He shook his
head.

"Can't. Waiting for that Army fellow to show
up about the cattle. I reckon Wesley can take good
care of you.''

"He's doing pretty well here, isn't he?"

"Seems to know what he's doing, sure
enough," Stacy replied.

"Who'll cook for you if I go?" she asked.

"Lemuel's coming in with the chuck wagon today," he said. "See. I have it all figured. You
might as well go and have a good time. You could
stay the night if you want.''

Martha thought it over and had to admit she
was tempted. It had been a long time since she
had talked with another woman. It had been a long
time since she had been in town, and there were
some things she needed.

"Okay, husband," she said. "I will go." He
nodded, satisfied. He liked to do nice things for
her too.

"Wesley'll be ready to go in about an hour,"
he said.

"So will I," she promised. He got to his feet and came over to her. He took her in his arms and gave her a long, gentle hug, then mumbled something about getting back to work and headed out the front door. She stood there motionless, and for quite a while she could still feel the warmth of his arms around her.

"See to it she comes to no harm," Stacy said to the man who was rapidly becoming his top hand. Wesley looked down on him from his saddle.

"No need to worry," he said. Stacy liked this man, liked his attitude and his careful ways. If Wesley said he didn't have to worry about Martha, Stacy believed him.

"If she decides to stay overnight, get yourself a room and stay too," he went on. "Whenever she comes back, you come back too."

"I understand everything you are saying," Wesley came back. "I even understand what you aren't saying." Stacy thought about that a minute, then grinned up at Wes.

"I am kind'a fond of her," he admitted. Wesley laughed.

"What a surprise," he said.

Martha came out of the house in her go-to-town outfit, a checkered gingham dress that somehow made her look like a younger girl than she really was. Stacy set the lunch basket in the back, then helped her into the buckboard, holding her just a second longer than necessary.

"Have a nice time," he said. "You need anything, you just ask Wesley." She smiled down at him.

"Don't worry so," she said. "I can take care of myself, you know." He looked at her for a minute then stepped back.

"You're burning daylight," he said, and they were on their way. Stacy stood and watched them as Wesley picked up the two ornery beeves from where Frank was keeping them contained. Then the woman he loved, the man he trusted, and two longhorns headed for town.

Yellow Knife sat astride his horse and looked out over the conclave. Even though he had been to the Sun Dance Ceremony before, never had he seen so many Indians all in one place. In a way, it was accidental.

The Sun Dance had gone well, with the great medicine man Sitting Bull presiding over the 400 tipis that made up the gathering. Once the dance was finished, the Indians stayed together as they moved along the river for almost another thirty days.

It was the season of new life, the time when everything grows again and the world turns green once more. It was the time of youth, as animals brought forth their young, when men and women, boys and girls, fell in love, and buds sprouted everywhere.

But it was not a time of carelessness, for these were not the years for careless Indians to survive, and so Yellow Knife had some of his young warriors out scouting for the whites. When they came riding into camp, warning of bluecoats, a council was called.

"They are following the river of the Sun Dance," Yellow Knife said. "If we do nothing, they will come upon our village. I do not think they are looking for peace," he added. Some of the other warriors smiled grimly. The bluecoats were not known to be looking for peace ever, unless it was on their terms.

"We can break camp and leave," said Sitting Bull. The others pondered on his words, for he was a wise and powerful man of medicine. Yellow Knife rose.

"I do not think the bluecoats would let us do that. I think they would come after us, for the lust of blood is in their hearts." He looked over the gathering, then went on. "We are many today. If we do not stop the bluecoats, tomorrow we may not be so many." He sat down and there was silence as his words were digested.

"If we try to stop the bluecoats, tomorrow we may not be so many also," said Sitting Bull.

Crazy Horse got to his feet and the attention

was turned on him as they silently waited for him to speak. He was well respected, perhaps better respected as a warrior chief than any other.

"I say that Yellow Knife speaks true," he said. "I shall take my warriors and drive back the bluecoats as the sun rises. They are careless and will not expect us to attack them. Many warriors will count coup tomorrow."

"I too agree with Yellow Knife," said Sitting Bull, finally. "I see a great victory for us tomorrow," and that was the way of the council.

In the morning well over six hundred warriors mounted their horses and rode into the rising sun. They attacked the bluecoats while they were still sitting around their cook fires drinking from their little metal cups. In a glorious battle that lasted the better part of the day, they killed more than twenty of the soldiers and wounded many more. Then Crazy Horse led them back to camp, but their number was less almost forty fine warriors who were now counted among the honored dead and whose names would be spoken no more. More than fifty others were bearing wounds from the battle, Yellow Knife among them.

He had been riding down on the desperate soldiers when a bullet sliced through the meat on his left shoulder. At first the feeling had been that of numbness and surprise. Then the blood began to flow and so did the anger in his heart. He had fought like a wild man, lust for enemy blood guiding his every move. No rational thought directed his actions. When he finally came back to the world of reality, his shoulder hurt and he had killed three soldiers with his own hands. His reputation as a warrior chief was now unsurpassed even by that of Crazy Horse.

The victory celebration waited, however, as the wise chiefs decided to move the village, and once they were safe near the mouth of the small creek, they staged their celebration, for the scouts reported the soldiers had turned tail and were headed away from them.

That had been six days ago, and their fellow Sioux, friends, and allies had been flowing into the village until it was now a thousand lodges large.

The tipis were arranged in typical circles of various tribes, with the Northern Cheyenne Circle of 120 tipis on the left. Stretched out to the right were the circles of the Hunpapa Sioux, Oglala Sioux, Minconjou Sioux, Sans Arc Sioux, and finally the Blackfoot, Brule, and Two Kettle Sioux Circle at the right end of the village.

The sight was something to make a man proud, and Yellow Knife had ridden up on the ridge across the river to look down at the massive gathering.

Because of the enormous quantities of food and

fuel such a village consumed, they had moved
back in the direction of the fight. The scouts had
reported antelope herds, and the village had followed the report until it reached the site that Yellow Knife appreciated this night.

Fully seven thousand Indians lay below him
basking in their tribal power. At least two thousand of them were full-fledged warriors. It was a
time of pride, but because of the massive demands
they made on food and fuel, it was a time that
could last but a few days at most.

Yellow Knife rode sedately down into the massive camp, down to his tipi and the food and love
of his woman. All was right with the world on
this evening. It was to get even better.

That night, as the crickets chirped and the smell
of fires wafted on the cool air, she lay next to him
under their buffalo robes.

"My husband," she said. He grunted, for he
was almost asleep.

"My husband," she repeated.

"What, woman?" he asked.

"Do you not get too alone sometimes?" she
asked. He stirred, annoyed.

"No," he said. "I have you to keep me warm,
and tonight I have many lodges circled around."

"I know," she said, "But in our life we have
but each other." Yellow Knife opened his eyes,
trying to figure out what she was saying.

Sometimes he was annoyed by how women could never say a thing straight out. It seemed like they always had to come at something from the side. It was sort of sneaky and not warriorlike.

"What are you trying to say?" he asked.

"You shall have a son," she replied, plain and direct. His eyes popped open wide in the night. He rolled over and looked at her dark form.

"You are with child?" he asked. He could see her nod and her teeth gleamed as she smiled at him.

"Yes, husband," she said. "You have sired a son. I can feel it is so."

Yellow Knife tried to maintain his warrior demeanor, but a smile split his face. He reached out for her and held her to him.

"That is wonderful," he said. She snuggled to his chest, as Yellow Knife grinned into the darkness. He held her close for quite a while, then he broke the wondrous silence.

"Perhaps," he said, "we should try for more than one." His wife giggled like a little girl and reached her soft arms around him.

Martha sat on the blanket and opened the picnic basket. Wesley sat on a rock across from her. His horse, Penny, saddle loosened, grazed contentedly beside the team from the wagon. The two longhorns were cornered in the arroyo behind them.

She took out a plate of fried chicken wrapped in a cloth and set it on the blanket, then brought out a jar of pickles and loaf of bread.

"Help yourself, Mr. Hader," she said. She brought out two glasses and a jar of water, which she proceeded to pour. Wesley came over, took one of the empty plates, and piled it full of food.

"Thank you, ma'am," he said, and went back to perch on the rock. Martha filled her own plate as she watched him eat.

Wesley dug in with vigor, but he never completely concentrated on his food. His eyes would flick from here to there as he kept watch on their surroundings. He worked on a chicken leg as he turned and examined their backtrail.

"You never really relax, do you, Mr. Hader?" she asked. His busy eyes flicked down to rest on her for a moment.

"Please, ma'am," he said, "I'd appreciate it if you would call me Wesley or Wes. Mr. Hader sounds so formal, almost like we were strangers."

"All right, Wesley," she said with a smile. "You didn't answer my question, though. You expecting trouble?"

"No, ma'am," he assured her. "Just that out here a man learns to be alert all the time. Just a habit, really. It has stood me in good stead on more than one occasion." He took a bite from his piece of bread. "I do not mean to make you nervous," he added.

Wesley took a moment to study this woman. She made *him* a little nervous if the truth be told. For one thing, she was the boss's wife. For another, she was a woman, and that was a form of life he did not understand hardly at all. Finally, she was darn pretty, what with her cute little nose with the band of tiny freckles across it, her crown of soft-looking hair, and her steady eyes.

Besides, she was his responsibility and he'd never been all the way accountable for a woman before. Stacy had given her care over to him, albeit temporarily, and a man could show no greater trust than that. Wesley had no desire to show up wanting when a man trusted him that much, so his attention was fine-tuned on everything that went on around them.

"Doesn't make me nervous, Wesley," she said. "It is just that I have seen that same look on another man just awhile back." She smiled a smile that spoke of her remembering something of which he had no part. Wesley looked at her for a moment and idly wondered what she was talking about.

The snake was large for a western diamondback, maybe five feet long, and thick with muscle. It had eaten but two days previously, a fat rabbit, and was not actively hunting yet, just sunning on the low rock. It had seen the motion from the longhorn grazing nearby, but the animal had been so far away it represented no threat. Somehow the beef got the notion that the grass was better over by the rocks, and it ambled straight over to where the reptile lay sunning on the rock.

The snake tightened into a coil and raised into the serpentine curve that precluded a strike. It hung there, tense in every muscle, and the sudden buzz of its rattle broke into the reverie of the warm afternoon. The longhorn, no stranger to rattlesnakes, decided that it was prime time to leave the general vicinity and did so posthaste. The other longhorn, also startled, joined in the rout, and it was a stampede of two that stormed right through the middle of the picnic and out into the rolling hills.

Martha sat motionless, eyes wide, as the two huge animals rushed by, knocking the picnic basket flying. By the time she realized she should move, the time for action was over and she turned to watch the two animals running into the grass, tails held out straight behind and flopping every which way as they ran.

"Dang!" she heard Wesley say as he yanked the cinch tight on Penny, then swung into the saddle and took off after the beeves.

"Be back shortly," he called over his shoulder, and then he was gone. Martha looked around slowly and ruefully examined the remains of her once-perfect picnic.

"Stupid cows," she mumbled, and began to pick up what was left of her dishes and food.

It took Wesley the better part of an hour to round up the two animals, and by then he had lost whatever fondness for them he had ever felt. They were independent and contrary and seemingly intent on heading in any direction except the one he wished them to go. He finally convinced them that he was the boss, at least temporarily, and they slowly walked back to the picnic site.

Martha was nowhere to be seen, but the mess had been carefully cleaned up and the broken picnic basket sat there lonesome-like and leaning to one side. The two beeves carefully stepped around it this time and ambled back into the arroyo, where they once again began to graze like nothing had happened.

"Go ahead and eat," said Wesley. "If you try to gct out of there again I swear I will have steak for supper for certain." They paid him no mind at all.

The snake, disturbed by all the previous activity, slowly moved out of the arroyo and came up on the horse suddenly. The two spotted each other about the same time, and Penny made that sudden sideways hop she always did when she saw a snake. Because of the quick hop, the bullet that should have killed Wesley caught him on the side of the head, slicing his scalp through to the skull and knocking him instantly unconscious. He fell backward from the saddle, landing on his back, blood streaming from his split scalp.

Penny moved nervously away to the side, and the snake crawled on, directly toward the unconscious man. Closer the snake slithered, and then it was upon him. The snake didn't even hesitate as it slid across the center of the still form, paying him no more attention than it would a rock or log. In a short time only moving grass told of the snake's progress into the land, and then that too was still. A bird sang a few tentative notes from the straggly tree. The two longhorns grazed contentedly, and in a few minutes Penny also dropped her head and began to eat.

Chapter Five

The morning was even better than the previous night for the father-to-be. Yellow Knife contemplated the joys and responsibilities of his impending fatherhood as he went through the routines of being a chief. Hunters were sent out to fill the always hungry bellies of his people, and several men were sent to see to their horses, now combined in the huge herd just west of the camp. Birds were singing and the sun marched slowly across the blue sky, peaked, and began the daily slide downward.

His wife was singing happily to herself as she went about her chores, smiling at him every time she caught his eye. Yellow Knife looked at the woman he loved. It was hard to believe she was carrying another person inside, his son. Sometimes life was too good.

He was one of the first to spot the dust cloud over the hill. He pondered on it for a moment, but it could only mean one thing. Many animals were moving over there. It could be almost anything, but his stomach grew hard and he knew.

"Get mounted and armed!" he called, and his warriors looked at him in surprise for a moment before they rushed to do as he had said. It took time to get their horses and weapons, and Yellow Knife could see dust from the camp of the Hunkpapas and Blackfoot as they too frantically prepared to fight the approaching enemy.

His men were among the first to be ready for battle, and he led them riding toward the enemy, for he could now see the lines of bluecoats.

They were coming at the Indians four across, in three separate groups, and even as he watched they dismounted, all except for one who could not control his horse and came running toward them. His actions were frantic as he tried to bring his horse under control, and many Indians fired their weapons at the rapidly advancing man but none hit. Yellow Knife could see the fear on the man's face as he sighted down the barrel of his beloved Henry and squeezed the trigger.

Private James Turley—Jim to his friends—took the bullet in the center of his chest. His fear was suddenly gone, and he blinked up into the swirling dust cloud, seeing the bright sun glaring down on him. The sounds of frantic men and running horses faded away as a feeling of silent peace came over him, and then he was still, the first man to die on that pretty afternoon.

Yellow Knife watched the bluecoats as every fourth man took three other horses and led them to the rear into the woods. The remaining soldiers knelt and began to fire at the Indians, the popping of their carbines adding to the noise and confusion.

"Follow me," Yellow Knife yelled, and led his mounted warriors along the length of the line of bluecoats, then curled around the end of the line to attack from the rear.

"Keep your young men alive!" It was as if Chief Stone Hand was speaking directly into his ear. Yellow Knife wanted to charge into the soldiers, to lay hands on the enemy, to count coup on them.

"Think with your heart and look over your feelings," Stone Hand said in his head.

Yellow Knife kept his warriors away from the bluecoats, content to ride up and down in their rear, firing into them from horseback. Here and there, a bluecoat would suddenly scream and fall.

Yellow Knife did not see how the enemy could stay where they were, and sure enough, they soon moved to their right, into the cottonwood groves. Hunkpapa and Blackfoot warriors also slipped on foot into the woods; others gathered on the other side of the river to fire their rifles at the bluecoats. Yellow Knife could not imagine what it must be like to be a bluecoat trapped in those woods, selling his life as best he could. He gathered his warriors to him.

"Let us charge in there!" said Crooked Fist, lust for battle plain on his face. "Let us kill them all!"

"They cannot stay in there," Yellow Knife responded. "Look at their position. They are spread out and will surely die if they do not get together and move."

"Then let us go in and kill them first!" insisted Crooked Fist.

"They will move," said Yellow Knife quietly and with certainty. "We will await them over there and when they come out, then we will attack. We will try to get in among them and kill them and count coup on as many as we can."

Some of his warriors were caught in the blood lust, but others were not anxious to tangle with the bluecoats and their carbines and maybe die. They assembled at the rear of the cottonwoods and waited for the promised retreat of the bluecoats to take place. Meantime they saw to their weapons and watched the relentless assault on the trapped men.

The fight was mass confusion in the woods, with men shooting and shouting and horses screaming in pain and fear. The bluecoat leader soon decided that his position was untenable, and true to Yellow Knife's prediction, the bluecoats came out the rear of the woods and mounted their horses once more. The soldiers spurred their animals into motion, and Yellow Knife led his men on a parallel path to their retreat, firing across their saddles into the soldiers. Many other Sioux were now mounted and riding with them, and they were also firing into the soldiers.

When Yellow Knife realized the bluecoats had left no rear guard to protect them, he led his mounted warriors right in among the fleeing enemy, closing on the panicked bluecoats and shooting or knocking them from the saddle almost at will. A part of him was wildly excited inside, thrilled and pleased to be the victor in so many man-to-man confrontations; another part was shocked at the carnage, dismayed at the waste of living men and animals under the hands of his warriors.

The bluecoats rode into the river, desperate to escape the attacking Sioux, and Yellow Knife pulled his warriors to a halt and had them fire from the banks into the struggling men in the water. Spouts of water would shoot into the air as bullets from his men missed the enemy, but not

all shots missed, and here and there a motionless body clad in blue would float facedown, drifting with the current in the peace of death.

Some of the bluecoats escaped the river and rode away into the ravines and up the bluffs.

"Let us cross and kill them too!" yelled Crooked Fist.

"Wait!" called Yellow Knife, shouting to make himself heard. "Listen." They could hear distant firing coming from the other direction.

"That is by our circle!" Yellow Knife said, thinking of his wife and his unborn son. "These bluecoats will gather together on the bluff and wait for us to return and kill them. For now, let us go and see what danger threatens our families."

It was unusual for warriors to follow the advice of leaders when they were fighting. It was normal for each man to answer his own call; to go at his own will and in his own time to do battle with the enemy. That was normal. Only Yellow Knife had proven to be so adept at fighting, so sparing with the lives of his men, that his warriors stayed with him and followed his bidding. He felt the great pride their obedience brought forth as they galloped toward the sound of the firing. It was still several hours until nightfall.

Wesley lay there for a minute, trying to figure out why he couldn't open his eyes. It was as if

they were stuck shut, as if someone had poured honey on them and the honey had dried into a crusty mess. He rubbed at his right eye with his fist as a small boy might do, feeling the crusty stuff break and crumble under his hand. When he tried to open it again, he pulled out an eyelash or two, but the red light of sunset poured in and he could see Penny off to one side watching him.

He got to his feet and staggered over to the patient horse, lifting his canteen from the saddle horn. Tilting his head back, he poured water on his face, then tugged the bandanna from his neck and wiped at the dried blood until he could see with both eyes once more.

Sundown. It was almost sundown. The two longhorns were grazing contentedly back in the arroyo, and the picnic basket stood crooked on the ground. Martha's wagon was still there, but there was no sign of the woman. Wesley gingerly felt the wound on his head while he tried to piece together what had happened.

Obviously he had been shot, but by whom he did not know . . . unless they had caught up with him, but after all this time it didn't seem likely. For sure it didn't seem likely that they would ambush him out here on Circle L land. But somebody sure had, and he couldn't think of anybody else who would have reason to shoot him from ambush like that.

He walked over to the basket, staggering a few times on the way. Something seemed wrong with his sense of balance, but he ignored it. He must find out what happened to Martha. The tracks around the wagon and basket told the tale plain as day.

Four men had come into the area around her. There had been a struggle, and one of them rode out with his horse carrying double. Wesley glared at the setting sun. In less than an hour it was going to be too dark to track them. He took the remaining food from the basket, stuffing the cloth-wrapped chicken into his saddlebags. Then, after two false starts, he swung up on Penny's back and rode along the evil men's tracks. He was so dizzy it was all he could do just to stay in the saddle. Every movement of the horse sent waves of nausea through him and even his tongue felt thick.

It was only a hundred yards until he found the empty case from a Henry rifle. It was hard to believe that anybody had missed killing him dead at that short range, but Wesley wasted no time marveling at his survival.

His head pounded every time his heart beat, but pain was not the emotion that drove him. Anger, red hot and acid in his belly, forced him onward. He swore on all he held dear that he would never quit following them until he found the evil perpetrators of this deed, until he brought them under his gun and killed them all. He would show them no mercy, for they had taken a helpless woman with them by force. He tried not to think about what might be happening to Martha. Besides, they had tried to kill him from ambush. The sun dropped inexorably lower in the sky.

He swayed in the saddle, sheer anger and will keeping him going. Finally, neither will nor anger was enough, and blackness swallowed him.

Penny stopped when the man fell from her back. She nuzzled at him once, and when there was no response, began to crop the grass around him.

Martha couldn't believe it was happening again. Once again she was being taken by force, taken from her home and hauled into the wilderness at the hands of a stranger. Only this time, there were four of them.

She was riding behind one called Marvin, a man of maybe fifty years. He hadn't said a lot to her, but she knew something of him and his past. His muscles were lean and hard under her hands where she held on as they rode, fast at first, then at a more leisurely pace. His clothing was that of a cowhand, complete down to his spurs, and he sat comfortable in the saddle. Only he was too old to be a cowhand. Probably a rancher, maybe with a place of his own. He didn't smell too good, either.

He did not have anything to say to her, and they rode in silence for hours until the sun began to set red in the west. Finally they stopped and the men set about making camp. Marvin looked at her.

"Cook," he said, and she did. Better to be busy and useful, she thought. It kept her from worrying about what was to come. As the coffee boiled, she thought about Stacy.

These men were as good as dead. Her husband would never quit looking and never quit coming until he caught up with them and killed them with that lightning-fast gun of his. Taking her was a mistake that would cost them their lives—sooner or later.

In the event that it was later, it was her job to stay alive until Stacy showed, no matter how long it took, no matter what she had to do. And so she cooked. Well, at least as best she could over the small fire they allowed her.

"Sure seems strange to have a woman around the camp," said the young one. "Watching her cook kind'a reminds me of back when Maw was alive."

The older one with the crooked teeth looked at the kid and grinned.

"She don't hardly remind me of Maw at all," he said in a tone that left no doubt about his train of thought. Martha felt fear surge through her, but fought it down as she fussed with the pans over the fire.

"Ain't gonna be none of that," Marvin said flatly. It was obvious he was the leader of the small band. "He up and killed my woman, now we done killed him and took his. Now it's for her to take on what Maw would'a done. That's justice, sure enough." He sat down on a rock and watched Martha cook. "No cause to think evil about her on account of I won't stand for it." Crooked Teeth dropped his eyes.

"Sure thing, Paw," he mumbled. Martha looked up at Marvin.

"I was not his woman," she said. "He was just going with me to town. He worked for my husband, who owns the Circle L Ranch." Marvin just looked at her and the silence dragged out. Martha poked at the beans with a fork, then looked up at him again.

"My husband will be coming after you just like you were following after Mr. Hader," she tried again. Nothing.

"Did you see how his head popped when my bullet took him?" the young one asked, almost excited. "I seen the blood fly real clear."

"A rifle bullet is a powerful thing, sure enough," said Crooked Teeth. "Only you should'a maybe shot him in the knees first and worked your way up. Too fast to shoot 'em in the head like that." He never took his eyes off Martha, and his steady gaze made her uncomfortable.

She spooned some beans onto one of the plates and took it to Marvin.

"He will be coming," she said softly. "He will kill you as sure as you're sitting there." Marvin never even looked at her as he took the plate and began to eat. It was like she wasn't there at all.

She got another plate and took it to Crooked Teeth.

"My husband will be coming," she said. "He will kill you for sure unless you let me go now." Crooked Teeth took the plate and looked up at her.

"My name is Buck," he said. "You should face up to it. Your man is dead on account of Johnny blew his head clean off." He grinned, displaying his twisted teeth, then dug his fork into the beans.

She took a plate to Johnny.

"You men are making a big mistake," she said as she handed him the food. "They don't look kindly on men who steal women out here, especially when they are married." Johnny looked troubled as he took the plate.

Paw?" he asked. Marvin never looked up from his plate, shoveling in the food.

"Don't pay her no mind, Son," he mumbled around a mouthful.

"But what if she's telling the truth?" Johnny asked. Marvin cackled.

"She's a woman, boy. Ain't no truth in her. She

just ain't real taken with our company yet.''
Johnny laughed.

"Okay, Paw," he said.

Martha took a plate over to the other man, re-alizing as she did so that she had never heard him speak. She studied him as she handed him the plate.

He was big, taller than Stacy even, and almost fat. His face had a pudgy boyish look, and the way his eyes met hers sent a shiver up her back. She realized he was not quite right in the head.

He took the plate in one hand and grabbed her wrist with the other. He had reached up so casu-ally, taking her wrist with no effort, but his raw animal power was incredible. Immediately her hand went numb.

She tried to pull away, but he held her fast, grinning at her vacantly, mouth agape.

"Let go!" she shouted. She heard Johnny laugh.

"Don't do no good to talk to Fred," Johnny said. "He can't hear nothin'. Can't talk neither. Just wait a minute and likely he'll let go."

Only he didn't let go. In a minute, he set the plate down and put his other hand on her arm and began to feel her arm, slowly moving his hand up past her elbow toward her shoulder. A string of drool leaked from the corner of his open mouth and began to trickle down his chin.

Outside, Martha stayed calm, but inside she was frantic. Just having his hands on her made her feel unclean, as if he was coating her arm with something dirty and slimy from a swamp. She didn't know what to do to get away from him. Her mind raced as his hand reached her shoulder. What would his mother have done? She reached out and patted him on the head gently. His hand stopped and he looked at her for a moment. Then he patted her on the head the same way. Suddenly, she was free.

Rubbing her wrist, she walked back to the fire and filled her own plate. When she looked up, Marvin was looking at her. He nodded slightly, then returned to his eating.

Martha was learning more about people the longer she lived. People were never all bad or all good. People were just people. They all wanted freedom and respect and love and justice. Sometimes their ideas of freedom and respect and justice were not always the same. For certain their thoughts about love were not always the same.

These four men were a family. They thought they had been wronged. Maybe they had, although she couldn't see Mr. Hader ever killing somebody's mother. They had reacted the way they felt was best, the way they believed gave them the justice they were entitled to have. It never entered their minds that they might be wrong in anybody else's eyes; probably they wouldn't have cared if they had thought about it. In their minds they were right. A wrong had been corrected.

She began to believe she could survive with these men. That was all she had to do. Survive.

She thought about Stacy and felt her eyes flood. She missed him and wanted his strong arms around her so much. Martha took a deep breath. Just hold on. Just keep thinking. Just survive. Stacy would be along. Maybe not tomorrow. Maybe not even soon. But one day, one day she would look up and he'd be there. Just survive until then.

She took the pot of beans and offered seconds to the four men.

Chapter Six

It was settled; the Army lieutenant had put his hand to it and even signed a paper, the paper Stacy laid flat on the desk and studied. One hundred head of cattle at twenty dollars each, delivered to Fort Ellis before July 30th. That came to two thousand dollars, more money than he had ever seen at one time. This, his first big sale, represented the salvation of the Circle L.

With two thousand dollars he could pay off Spivey at the store, Frank at the lumber mill, and Mr. Waulk at the bank. There would even be money left over to see them through the rapidly approaching winter. He wanted to add on to the barn, improve the bunkhouse, and let Martha spruce up the inside of the house. Wouldn't hurt

70

to put on another room either. That was a mighty lot of change in a man's life just from a single piece of paper.

Not that he was flat broke exactly. He had almost two hundred dollars put away in a sock, but that was needed money, needed to pay his cowhands and buy whatever they had to have. 'Course, now he could spend it, since he could see more coming in pretty soon.

The dickering had actually been enjoyable. The lieutenant was young, maybe twenty-five or so, but his manners had been impeccable. Stacy had ridden out with the man and showed him the beeves on the range and the lieutenant had immediately begun talking down the size and deformities of Stacy's cattle. 'Course, Stacy became busy talking up the fat and tenderness of the meat, and they had continued the friendly bickering over Lemuel's supper. After three games of checkers, they had agreed on the twenty dollars a head they had both expected would be the final price all along.

The lieutenant had spent the night in the bunkhouse; in the morning they had drawn up the paper, both had signed, and the lieutenant had gone on his way. All in all, it had been a pleasant social affair in Stacy's rather spartan existence.

It had sure seemed strange for him to be alone in that bed. Even though they had only been married four months, it was as if he couldn't remember being alone ever, as if Martha had always been a part of his life. No doubt in his mind she always would be. He missed her, and he hoped she was having a good time with her friend Alice.

"Hey, Boss!" he heard Frank yell from out front. "Better get out here now!" Stacy grabbed his gunbelt, swung it around him, and began fumbling with the buckle as he headed for the door. Frank never yelled, and if he did now, that meant trouble.

Frank was standing out there with his hand shading his eyes against the morning sun. Stacy looked in the same direction and made out two horses coming over the bluff toward the ranch. He squinted into the brightness. The front one was the lieutenant sure enough. Something was not quite right with the second horse and rider.

Stacy felt the hair on the back of his neck stand up. It was Wesley's horse the lieutenant was leading, and there was a man draped across the saddle. Stacy thought about that and felt himself go numb all over. There was no sign of Martha.

The lieutenant was coming at a slow walk, and inside Stacy wanted him to hurry up. 'Course, the slow walk meant that he was trying to be gentle with Wesley, which meant the man must still be alive. No need to be gentle with the dead. Stacy forced himself to stand there patiently, waiting for the two to ride up. He wasn't even aware that he was tying his gun down while he waited. The lieutenant rode up.

"This man belong to you?" he asked as he swung down.

"He does," said Stacy as Frank eased Wesley out of the saddle.

"He took a mighty hard knock in the head," said the lieutenant. "Lucky to be alive, I'm thinking."

"Put him in the house," Stacy told Frank, and Frank half walked, half carried Wesley up to the door.

"Mr. Leech," Wesley said weakly. Stacy was right there.

"Where is she, Wes?" he asked.

"I can't hardly see," Wesley said, "or I'd be tracking them myself."

"Tracking who, Wes?" Stacy asked harshly. "Who took her?"

"Four men," Wesley said. It was as if he couldn't keep his knees stiff and straight. First one would buckle under him, then the other.

"They ambushed me," he went on. "Missed me at a hundred yards with a Henry. I was trackin' them when I passed out like a girl. Just give me a few minutes and I'll be ready to go with you."

"Put him in bed in the house and have Lemuel see to him," Stacy said. "Obliged, Lieutenant," he said. The lieutenant turned his horse.

"Good luck, Mr. Leech," he said, and moved out once more.

Stacy went into the house and threw some supplies together. He took the money from the sock, counted out $120, and gave it to Frank.

"Pay off the boys," he said. Frank opened his mouth to speak, then said nothing as Stacy took two boxes of rifle shells and two boxes of .45s and headed out the door.

In less than ten minutes, Stacy rode out. He never looked back at the ranch he had worked so hard to build. He never looked back at the ranch he would now lose.

He cut their trail about noon. They were almost a full day ahead of him. Off in the west, thunder rumbled and promised one of the warm summer rains. Despair settled on him like a weight on his shoulders. It was going to rain and wash away their tracks before he could ever catch up with them. He marked their direction of travel. Southeast.

Clouds loomed ever lower overhead and thunder grew louder and closer. Stacy pulled his hat down tighter and slipped into his long coat as he rode steadily in the tracks of the men who had taken his wife.

Martha woke at the first light. She had not slept well, but every time she had awakened and looked around, one of the brothers had been standing guard on the camp, and they had all been alert. No chance to escape. Maybe later.

Sleeping on the ground was very unpleasant for her. She had been used to that big, soft bed, with Stacy warm and strong alongside. The ground was hard and full of little pebbles that seemed to work through the blanket and grow larger as the night progressed. Besides, there had been the constant dripping of rain through the cracks in her lean-to, drops of cool water that plopped down on her blanket and made wet places that grew in size as the night went on.

She felt dirty and definitely in an evil spirit, but she swallowed her distress and rolled out of the makeshift bedroll. At least it hadn't been too cold, and the bright morning sky promised a warm day to come.

Fred was siting there on guard, rifle across his lap. He watched her pat at her hair. Martha smiled at him but elicited no response from the big man-child. He watched carefully as she went off into the scruffy bushes, but made no move to stop her. When she returned, the others were beginning to stir in their bedrolls.

Martha built up the fire and put the coffeepot on to boil. When she looked up, Marvin was looking at her.

"Morning," she said. He nodded back, but she

could easily see the distrust in his eyes. He would do well to distrust her. She would try to escape at the first opportunity. Failing that, she would sooner or later get her hands on a weapon. When she did, Marvin was going to let her go free or she would shoot him. She had no doubt she would be able to pull the trigger on him or his sons if need be.

Even if she never got a weapon, even if she never escaped, there was always Stacy. He was coming. She could feel him back there somewhere, feel his anger at these men. He would come. He would never stop looking. He would find her. Then he would kill Marvin. He would kill Buck with his crooked teeth, and Johnny with his youthful innocence, and even Fred with his babyfat face and stupid ways. And then they would go home and leave these men behind.

Martha sliced bacon into the skillet and looked across the fire at the four men. She wouldn't mind seeing them dead, and the feeling surprised her. She had always disliked violence. Of course, that was before these men had killed Mr. Hader and stolen her away from the man she loved.

"Morning, Martha," said Johnny as he gave her a bright smile.

"Morning, Johnny," she responded. "Breakfast in a few minutes." Johnny sniffed at the morning air.

"Sure smells good," he said. "I'll be right back." With that he pulled on his boots and headed out into the bushes.

One at a time the others arose, pulled on their boots and hats, then made the morning trek into the bushes. Martha watched them without seeming to watch them.

They didn't seem so powerful, so evil, so bad in the morning. They just seemed like tired men, not yet wanting to rise, men who yawned and acknowledged her presence, yet presented no real immediate threat. They stretched and tendons snapped and they groaned. Johnny rubbed at his eyes like a small boy, and Buck took a small stick and brushed at his crooked teeth. Only Fred remained motionless, alert, watching. The rifle looked like a small toy as it lay on his lap.

Martha spooned out some beans and bacon onto a plate and took it over to Marvin. He grunted thanks and watched her as she took food to his sons before taking a plate for herself. Fred ate as he kept watch. Martha had given him his plate and then, on impulse, patted him on the head as she had the night before. Fred had patted her right back, but had done it absently, for he was watching the horizon, taking care of his family.

She ate only half her food before she took the skillet around to give seconds to the men. Marvin took another plateful, all the while watching her.

"Won't do you no good to try and hold us back," he said. "Ain't nobody coming after us."

"I just thought you might want more food," she said, covering up her dismay that she had been so transparent. "But there *is* somebody coming after us," she went on. "My husband is back there somewhere, and he will never stop until he finds me."

Marvin shoveled a forkful of beans into his mouth and chewed slowly.

"Makes you feel better to say that, why, you go on ahead," he finally said, mouth full. "Even if'n there was somebody back there, they'd never be able to track us after all that rain. Mind, we changed directions a couple a' times yesterday." He swallowed. "If I thought you really did have a husband back there, why, I'd let you go for sure. Only I think you are likely lying on account of you are a woman and do not know no better." He scooped up another forkful and stuffed it in. Obviously, the conversation was over.

Martha turned to go back to her own food, and a bleat of fear escaped her lips. Fred was standing there, huge and solid, directly in front of her. She had never heard him come up behind her at all. Marvin snorted a laugh at her surprise.

She stepped aside and looked up at the puffy face of the man-child. He was looking at Marvin, looking at his Paw, with a look of want on his face. Marvin seemed to understand him, nodded easy, and reached out for the rifle. Fred grinned, handed Marvin the rifle, and practically ran into the bushes, slipping his suspenders down as he left. Marvin and Martha exchanged solemn stares.

"Has Fred always been like that?" she asked. Marvin took a bite and worried it for a while as if he was pondering on his answer.

"Born that way," he said. He looked up at her, his face carved in stone, yet she could see a touch of shame. Pain was there also.

"Bad seed, I guess," he mumbled as he took another bite. His eyes dropped from hers. Martha could think of nothing to say, so she went back to her plate and her beans, which were already cold.

Her fork had a bent tine, and it felt weird, sort of off-center, when she put it in her mouth. The beans were pretty good, though, because she had been liberal with the molasses and sugar. She scooped them from the metal plate and swallowed them down. Best that she keep her strength for later.

Fred came back into the camp, moving fast. His pants were held up with only one suspender, the other hanging down his left leg. He was holding his right wrist with his left hand. Even though he made no sound, could make no sound, not a person in camp did not know he was in distress. His face was twisted up as if he was going to cry.

Marvin jumped to his feet but Fred ignored him, coming straight toward Martha instead. He stopped in front of her and held out his meaty hand for her to study. Martha found herself on her feet waiting for the big man-child.

The two puncture wounds on the back of his hand were easy to see. A small drop of blood trembled over one of them. Snake bite. Big snake too, because the wounds were pretty far apart.

Martha wasted a second looking in Fred's eyes. The big man looked down at her, eyes pleading and afraid, lower lip trembling just short of tears. For the first time, it really sank in to Martha that Fred really was just a boy in a man's body—a very young boy in a very large man's body.

She reached up, took the bandanna from his neck, and tied it around his arm halfway between the wrist and the elbow. She tied it tight, but not like a tourniquet. She could feel Marvin standing behind her.

"Oh, lord!" Marvin said when he caught sight of Fred's hand. The pain in his voice was easy to hear. It was the pain of a father who loved his son regardless of the boy's problems, the voice of a father unable to help his boy when his boy needed it most. It was a voice a frontier woman heard all too often in the wilderness.

"Help him," Marvin said, and he was so close behind her she could smell his sour breath.

"You'd better help him or else!" he hissed, voice hard and angry. Martha turned on him.

"What kind of a person do you think I am?" she said angrily. "I will do what I can for him, and damn you for thinking otherwise! Now get away from me, and do it now!"

It was the first time she had seen him evidence any kind of emotion at all, and it might have been funny had the situation not been so serious. His eyebrows rose toward his hairline in surprise, and for a moment, the small boy in him came forward, the scolded small boy caught with his hands in the cookie jar. He took two steps back from her anger.

"Yes'm," he said. "Sorry." He turned to go.

"Wait," Martha said and he stopped as if he had been shot. "Give me your knife."

Marvin never hesitated as he took his big bowie from the sheath and handed it over.

Martha tugged gently on Fred's arm, and he sat on a rock in front of her. His eyes never left hers, and she could hear him screaming silently in her head as he held his injured hand up for her ministrations.

"It'll be all right, Fred," she said softly, even knowing he couldn't hear her. Somehow, it was as if he could understand anyway, and she kept crooning gently to the big man-child.

"You'll be okay, Freddie. You'll be okay."

His eyes never left hers, even as she made the

awful but necessary incisions over each fang mark. His blood flowed freely, dripping from his hand to soak into the wet ground at their feet.

"One of you chew some tobacco," she ordered. Marvin bit off a chaw and began to chew.

Martha loosened the bandanna and let the wounds bleed freely for a while. Anything to get the venom out of him.

"Come here, Marvin," she said, and he meekly came up to her, chewing furiously. She held out the bandanna.

"Here," she said. He looked at her a moment, then deposited the wad of wet tobacco in the center of the cloth. Martha put the wet stuff directly on the gaping wounds and tied the bandanna tight around Fred's hand.

"There," she said. "That's the best I can do for him. We have to get to a doctor." She looked at Marvin.

"Nearest one is in Fort Ellis," he said. "'Bout a full day's ride." Martha shook her head.

"He shouldn't ride if we can help it. We should keep him as quiet as possible." She thought a minute. "Maybe a travois." Marvin thought about that for a minute, then looked skeptical.

"You trying to hold us back?" he asked. "Put him on a horse and we can get there quicker."

"If you put him on a horse, only three of us will make it there at all," she said. "Now you three make a travois and do it now.'' She looked at Fred. ''Better make it a big one too,'' she said. Marvin studied her for a moment, then nodded, and the three men got to work. She turned to her patient.

Fred was sweating, face pale. She slid up his sleeve and the sleeve of his long underwear. Already a few small red blotches showed where the poison was working on his arm. She looked in his eyes and he gazed back, pleading with her. She nodded gently.

''Okay, Fred,'' she said. ''You'll make it okay.'' He looked a little relieved. He seemed to understand her; maybe it was her expression. She tried to look calm and sure, but inside she wasn't calm and sure. She pulled his big head to her and held it against her, trying to comfort the scared little boy inside.

Fred could very well die. It didn't depend on her. It didn't depend on the doctor. Actually, it depended on the snake.

Sometimes snakes didn't waste their poison. Sometimes they just bit and the people they bit showed no problem at all, or maybe just some minor troubles. Maybe this snake had just put a little poison into the big man. Maybe the snake hadn't shot Fred full with the nasty stuff. Maybe.

Martha was a little surprised at herself. Last night this man had scared her to death. She brushed some of the wet hair back from his forehead. Now she was hoping he would not die. Fred kept turning to look up at her, eyes pleading for comfort and release from his fear. She didn't mind. She patted him gently on the head and let her hand rest there. He looked at her like a grateful puppy, and she smiled at the sick boy-man.

She wondered what Stacy would say if he could see her taking care of one of her captors. It would be a shame to save this boy's life only to have her own husband shoot him dead. The thought bothered her some, so she put it back in her mind and forgot about it. Cross your bridges as you come to them. That seemed like real wisdom, especially now.

Chapter Seven

Yellow Knife could not get over the feeling of loss. Crooked Fist, the best friend he ever had or probably ever would have, was dead. The bluecoat with the dark hair under his nose had raised up, aimed his rifle, and put a bullet right through Crooked Fist. His friend had fallen backward off his horse and bounced on the ground, arms flying every which way. Yellow Knife himself had ridden down the soldier, knocking him flat on the ground with his horse, then firing the Henry into the bluecoat three times. The bluecoat was dead, but so was Crooked Fist, and they were probably together in the afterlife, two warriors, one not much different from the other.

He watched his people moving on as he sat on

his faithful war pony. The tribe was back to normal size, the large gathering broken up and scattering in all different directions as each individual chief saw fit. Stone Hand's old wife walked past, and Yellow Knife wondered if the old chief was with Crooked Fist. Maybe they were watching him right now and judging him with each decision he made. Maybe the bluecoat was with them too. He sighed and looked on his people, men, women, and children whose very lives depended on decisions he would make and maybe had already made. It was not easy being a chief. He booted his horse into motion and joined the straggling band of Sioux.

The bluecoats had been stopped. Indeed, many had been killed. But it was not a victory without cost. Many warriors had gone with Crooked Fist into the sky. Many lodges were singing the songs of mourning. It was probably the same in the bluecoats' fort, or at least it would be when the news of the great battle finally reached there.

The thing that bothered Yellow Knife the most about the whole battle, aside from the death of Crooked Fist, was that he suspected the bluecoats would now chase the Sioux without letup. Their hearts would be full of vengeance, and they would not rest until the Sioux were but a memory on the lonely land. He had said as much during the great council after the battle, but other's blood still ran hot with the wonder of battle and they had not listened to him as they celebrated the victory.

"We have won the battle," he said. "But I think we will lose our land and maybe our very lives because of it." Some of the others had even laughed. Crazy Horse himself had laughed, but Sitting Bull had been serious and even nodded slightly. Yellow Knife had sat down and kept his silence after that, but later, as they were watching the dancing, Sitting Bull had come to him and spoken with him. Sitting Bull was the greatest of medicine men, and Yellow Knife had been surprised to suddenly find him talking softly in his ear.

"You were right, Yellow Knife," Sitting Bull had said. "With this victory we have lost the Sioux nation. Do not judge the others harshly. Let them have this time of joy, for this will be the last victory dance of the Sioux." Yellow Knife had looked at the medicine man. His face was serious and his eyes glistened in the firelight.

"It is for each chief to decide the fate of his own people now," Sitting Bull went on. "You have proven yourself to be a warrior among warriors. Your heart is brave and strong. You must decide for your people how they will be remembered. Brave but dead is not to be feared," he went on, "but there is much to be said for crafty and alive." Yellow Knife could hear the subdued wailing of mourning from some of the lodges, even over the noise of the celebration.

"I will think on your words," he said to Sitting Bull. The medicine man turned away.

"I know you will," came Sitting Bull's words back over his shoulder, "else I would not have wasted them," and then he was gone, swallowed up by the revelers.

His thoughts were brought back to the present as a rider galloped up to him. It was Two Dog, one of the men posted as scouts ahead of the column.

"We have crossed the trail of some whites," he said. "Four men, one of them very large, and one woman. They have but four horses, and the woman rides with one of the men."

"Are they bluecoats?"

"No. Just men and one woman," came the answer. Yellow Knife nodded. Two Dog waited for a while to see if his chief was going to say more, then rode off to one side as his chief thought on the new development.

Some of the young women watched Two Dog as he rode there straight and proud. They watched him because it was an honor for a warrior to be selected scout. They watched him because he had shown himself to be brave in the recent battle. Mostly they watched him because he had not yet taken a wife.

Yellow Knife considered the information. Four men and a woman with the woman riding double. It was interesting and roused his curiosity. It would be intriguing to find out more about them. He could feel the old chief looking over his shoulder, and he did not let his feelings take him over but reasoned the problem through completely.

If he sent his warriors after the whites, his young men would doubtless kill them. While this meant four more horses for his tribe, it also meant his people would attract the attention of the many bluecoats certain to come. Better to let the whites live and lose the four horses than become the focus of the bluecoats' anger. Still, it would be interesting to know about them, know what they were doing out here, where they were going and why. He motioned Two Dog over and the warrior rode knee-to-knee with his chief.

"We will let them be for now," Yellow Knife said. Two Dog showed no reaction, but Yellow Knife could tell he was disappointed. "Killing them would only attract the attention of the bluecoats who will still be angry because of their loss at Greasy Grass." Better to explain the decision than have any of his men go off and kill the whites in spite of his command.

"The bluecoats will be as many as the stars in the sky," he went on. "Better to let some other tribe be the focus of their anger."

Two Dog thought on his words, then nodded in agreement. He was brave. He was not weak in the head.

"You can watch them for a while," Yellow Knife said. "Then come back and tell me what you have discovered."

Two Dog's face lit up and he nodded in agreement. It was exactly the kind of adventure a young warrior craved. Yellow Knife himself would have dearly loved to go and watch the whites.

Two Dog rode off. Several of the young women turned their heads to watch him go.

Two Dog was not unaware of the young women's attention, but it would not be warriorlike to pay any heed. He was flattered, however, especially when he saw that Eye of Fawn was looking at him. She was the woman who walked in his mind even when he did not wish her to be there, even when he was fighting the bluecoats. After he had killed the bluecoat with the broken leg, he had rested for a moment and looked for another to fight, and Eye had come into his mind. That was not good. A warrior could die that way, but he could not keep her away and, in truth, had no wish to. He could feel her eyes on him, or thought he could, until he was out of sight.

This watching of the whites would be more than interesting, and was the kind of assignment that any warrior would love. He would dearly like to single them out and kill them one by one, for that would add four horses to his wealth, but Yellow Knife had spoken smart and true. Two Dog could see the reason for not killing the whites. It would be better to have the angry bluecoats concentrate on some other tribe.

He kicked his pony into a canter and rode on the trail of the four men and one woman.

Stacy reined in and studied the scene. The trail was plain. Indians. Many Indians. It was obviously a village on the move, and not more than several hours ahead. They were also proceeding in a southwesterly direction, obliterating any faint remnants of the trail made by Martha's abductors. Doubtless, the Indians knew about the four whites ahead of them, and chances were more than fair that they would attempt to kill or capture them. He put down the almost overpowering sense of despair and studied the terrain.

The tribe was moving through a natural valley that continued for many miles. More than likely, Martha and those evil men were doing the same. To get around the Indians would require going around the mountains, and that would take more time than he could spare, maybe two or three days. The only other alternative was to try to make it around by going up on the ridges and passing them close by. It was barely possible to travel up there . . . maybe. It would not be pleasant. If the Indians posted sentries on the mountains, not very likely in his opinion because only a crazy man would try to travel up there, he would probably wind up dead.

His big mare, Ruby, hesitated, then began to climb, picking her footing carefully. In less than an hour he was walking and leading her on the narrow ledge that he hoped would widen out farther up the valley.

When the travois broke it startled everybody, the left log breaking with a crack like a rifle shot. Fred rolled off the travois, rolling on his swollen arm. When Martha got to him, silent tears of pain were running down his face. His agonized expression told of his suffering. She shook her head in pity.

"Must be pretty awful not to be able to scream when you want to," she said to nobody in particular as she and Marvin tried to comfort the hurt man-child. Martha knelt beside him and put her arm around Fred's wide shoulders. She could feel him trembling with weakness, fear, and pain.

"That'd only be a small part of the awfulness of his affliction," Marvin said softly as he watched her comfort his boy. Martha looked up at him as she hugged and rocked the desperately sick creature that was Marvin's son. Marvin surprised her with the humanity of his statement, and once again she had a brief glimpse into his tortured soul as he took full blame for the pain and suffering endured by his son as a result of his own weak seed.

Buck and Johnny went looking for another travois pole. Two Dog watched from behind some rocks, confident that the whites had no idea he was there. They were not being very careful. Of course they had that sick man, snakebite most likely, to worry about. It seemed fairly obvious they were going to take him to the small fort a day away.

The tribe was not very far back, moving fast as they were, and it looked as if these whites would be overtaken within the hour if they didn't get moving again. Two Dog thought that would make for an interesting situation, and he lay there, still as part of the rock while time drifted away.

The two men came back with a tree and set about trimming off all the branches to make another travois pole. Two Dog could hear the approach of the tribe, but the whites were making too much noise, what with their chopping and talking, to notice the approach of more than one hundred Indians moving fast.

Yellow Knife was around the curve and down on the whites before either of the two groups had any inkling that their lives were about to take a sudden detour. Behind him the tribe followed along in the usual disorganized but surprisingly efficient fashion. When Yellow Knife pulled his horse to a halt, he was not ten feet from the whites, and he stopped so suddenly that the tribe behind split on him like water on a rock and flowed around in a ragged bunch of men and women until they too stopped. It was hard to say who was more surprised, but Two Dog doubtless enjoyed the encounter more than any of them.

Martha's eyes widened and her hand went to her mouth in shock as many, many Indians suddenly appeared around her where there had been nothing but wilderness before. Shock piled up on shock as she recognized the leader as the Indian who had once before made her his prisoner.

Yellow Knife sat there motionless, looking down on the whites as more of his tribe shuffled around the encircled whites and looked at them in silence. The older white man stood there, mouth open wide in shock, and his expression, along with those of his sons, was enough to make some of the women giggle. The whites stood absolutely motionless as the Indians began to talk among themselves, quietly at first, then more excitedly, with laughter from many.

Yellow Knife glanced at the woman holding the sick man around the shoulders, then snapped his gaze back to her as he recognized her. He was astonished, but did not let it show.

''It is truly a small land,'' he said, but of course

she did not understand him. He turned to his people.

"Have Light One come forward," he said; there was a shuffling among the people and Light One stepped forward. He looked at the whites, then up at his chief.

"You wanted me?"

"I want you to speak to the whites for me," Yellow Knife explained. Light One nodded.

"I will try," he said.

"Tell the woman that it is a small land," said Yellow Knife. Light One looked puzzled, but turned to the woman.

"Chief Yellow Knife stated the land is not large," he said.

Martha was more astonished than before if that was possible. The Indian was speaking English! She thought about the words. The chief must have recognized her.

"Not large and sometimes crowded," she said. Light One repeated that to Yellow Knife. Yellow Knife stared at her for a moment, then the corners of his mouth turned up in a small smile that vanished instantly.

Two Dog rose from his cluster of rocks and came up to his chief.

"Let us kill them and move on," he said. "They will not be found."

"This is probably true," said Yellow Knife,

"but they might be of more value to us as prisoners."

Two Dog thought about that. Everybody knew the story of how Yellow Knife got his wonderful Henry rifle.

"As you say," he said to his chief, then turned and walked out to get his horse.

Some of the braves relieved the whites of their weapons and tied their hands. When they got to the woman, Yellow Knife waved them off.

"She will walk with me for a while," he said, "For I know her." The other Indians were surprised. "This is the woman I traded for my rifle," he explained.

Martha couldn't understand the attitude of the Indians. They were obviously taking them prisoner, being none too gentle with the men, but they seemed almost friendly to her. Two braves took her by the arms and led her beside the chief's horse, then left her.

"What of the large one on the travois?" Yellow Knife was asked.

"What is wrong with him?" he asked.

"He was bitten by a snake," came the answer, "on the hand." Yellow Knife considered the problem.

"Bring him along," he said. "If his horse cannot keep up, we will leave him." He turned to Light One.

"Light One, you will ride with me and I will speak with the woman through you."

"As you wish," from Light One. "I think you should put her on a horse," he went on. "I am certain she cannot keep up with our women walking."

"Bring one of the horses that belonged to the whites," Yellow Knife said. "But first tell her that she belongs to me now and that if she tries to ride away I will have my braves catch her and then she will belong to them."

Light One explained to Martha in broken English. She nodded understanding. She looked at the many braves clustered around their chief. There would be no attempt on her part to escape.

She mounted the horse they brought her, Yellow Knife booted his horse into motion, and they were moving once more. When Martha turned in the saddle, she could see Buck, Marvin, and Johnny walking in a line, hands tied, a rope from one neck to the other. Fred was back among the women on the travois. They rode in silence for more than an hour.

"Ask her what happened to the man," Yellow Knife said. Light One translated.

"He is my husband now," Martha explained. "We have a ranch in that direction." She pointed behind them. "We raise cattle." A thought entered her head. "Chief Yellow Knife is welcome to some of our cattle each year so he can jerk beef for the winter,'' she said. It was a lot to translate, and she wondered just how it came out in Sioux.

"How many cattle?'' came the reply. Martha thought that over. It looked like there were about a hundred and fifty in his tribe.

"Five,'' she said.

"Ten,'' came the blunt reply.

"Seven.'' She knew Indians loved to barter.

"Nine.''

"Seven.''

"Nine.''

"Eight,'' she said.

"Eight,'' came the answer. They rode in silence again and Martha began to feel some hope for her situation. Yellow Knife spoke to Light One, who turned to her.

"Chief Yellow Knife says he can take the cattle anyway. If your husband tries to stop us, we will kill him.'' His eyes studied her face, and Martha tried not to let her disappointment show. Yellow Knife had just been toying with her, like a cat with a mouse. She kept her face bland and expression-less, but inside she felt herself sinking into the quagmire of despair.

She tried to remember everything she had ever heard about what the Indians did with captive women. As far as she could recall, a life of slavery and drudgery would be the best she could hope for. She considered attempting to ride away; maybe a quick death would be the best that could happen to her. Then she remembered. Maybe she would not die. Maybe she would end up belonging to all his braves. Maybe she would only be able to wish she was dead.

She rode in silence beside the chief. It was then that she noticed Light One was wearing an Army coat. Seventh Cavalry, it said. She wondered how he had obtained the coat, then decided she didn't really want to know.

Chapter Eight

It was midafternoon when they rounded a curve in the valley and came upon the line of rocks. There were seven of them, not too large, and they were in a straight line across the trail. They spelled out a clear message to Yellow Knife. Go no farther. He reined in and looked around.

They were in the narrowest part of the valley, a place where the floor funneled down to less than two hundred yards wide. Since Two Dog had not reported anybody ahead, the rock movers must be on the ridges where they could shoot down into the tribe as they passed. He had not thought anybody could be on the ridges. He had obviously been wrong, and he could imagine Stone Hand shaking his head in disgust.

100

Stacy watched from his perch above the Indians. He could see Martha riding alongside the chief. Relief flooded through him. She was alive and well, at least so far. The four men who took her from him were captives, although it appeared one of them had been hurt and was in a travois.

The chief looked around, looking up the walls of the canyon. His eyes reached the point where Stacy lay, and stopped there. For a moment Stacy felt uneasy, almost as if the Indian could tell he was there, then the man's eyes moved on. With a shock, Stacy realized who the Indian was.

This time, however, the situation was different. Stacy was not trying to keep from being discovered or avoiding conflict. This time, Stacy had the advantage, for that Indian had his women and children along. The Indian chief was not looking for trouble, but he had found it for sure. He was going no farther until Martha was released, no matter how many of them Stacy had to kill. He readied himself. The first Indian across that line of rocks was a dead Indian. Then the chief did the one thing Stacy hadn't counted on. He slid from his horse and sat down on one of the rocks.

The chief spoke a few words, and the rest of the tribe busied themselves with lighting cooking fires and settling down for a rest. Martha too got down from her horse and stood by the chief. She kept looking up in the rocks—looking for him, most likely.

Martha had seen the line of rocks too. She felt a flood of warmth gush through her. It had to be Stacy. She kept looking up the rock walls, looking for her man. He was up there somewhere. She desperately wanted to see him, and at the same time tried to beg him to stay out of sight and away from the Indians. He was probably looking down on her at this very moment, and she felt his eyes, or thought she did.

Stacy lay there in the rocks not three hundred yards from the woman he loved, watching the Indians in frustration. He had been all keyed up, ready to fight, ready to kill, but it was now postponed until the Indian chose to start the action. Control had been taken away from him. He had underestimated the chief down there. It would not happen again.

He was certain the chief had sent some of his warriors up on the ridges to hunt out and kill the man or men who were annoying him. Stacy could almost feel them coming after him. Every now and then Martha would look up to the walls, looking for him, most likely. It was only three hundred yards, but it might as well be three hundred miles.

He wasted a minute looking down on her, then forced her from his mind. Their survival depended on him outthinking the Indian, and she was for sure a distraction that interfered with clear thinking.

One mile back, White Feather found the scuff marks of Stacy's trail, marks where a white man's horse with metal shoes had scraped on the bare rock of the narrow ledge. He could see the brush marks where the white man had tried to brush his trail away with a piece of bush, for a single green leaf caught in a small crack betrayed the white man's effort. He looked ahead, but the trail narrowed even more and curved around the face of rock.

There was only one man ahead, at least on this side of the canyon, but this single man had stopped the whole tribe and must be killed or captured. His chief had asked that the white man be taken alive if possible, but White Feather had already made up his mind that the white man would die. His death would bring honor to the lodge of White Feather, not to mention another horse and some new weapons.

White Feather looked over the edge of the ledge. It was a long way down to the ground, and he was not happy with heights, but the white man was ahead and he would be careful. If anybody went off the edge, it would not be him. At least he didn't have to worry about the security of the trail since the white man and his horse had passed this way before.

White Feather hurried up to the curve in the trail, then slowed down. It would not be good to blunder around that curve. If the white man was watching for somebody on his backtrail, that would be an ideal place for an ambush. White Feather studied the cliff. There was no other route around the curve.

He lay down on his belly and slithered up, straining to see around the warm rock. He stuck his head around the edge of the rock, then drew it back very fast. He had seen nothing but more trail. No sign of the white man. He gave another brief look and saw nothing. Of course, that did not mean that the white man was not hiding behind a rock out there somewhere. He could be watching, waiting for somebody on his backtrail, waiting with his rifle ready, finger on the trigger.

Another quick look, then another, longer this time. Nothing. There was a good-size rock down the trail nestled up against the cliff face, but it was not likely the white man could be hiding behind that rock. It seemed more likely that the white was sure nobody could track him on this bare rock. It seemed more likely that the white was not watching his backtrail, not worried about it at all.

White Feather stood and showed himself around the curve, then suddenly stepped back. He had been hoping to draw a shot if the white man was there, but only silence greeted his movement. White Feather suddenly looked over the edge.

The stragglers of his tribe were down there, and several of the women were looking up, laughing, watching him. Inside he fumed at them for drawing attention to his location on the ledge. One of the warriors down there made some talk at the women, and they turned away from him and ignored him. He wondered if they had seen his fearful approach to the curve, wondered if they were laughing at him, questioning his courage and spirit.

The thought brought a flood of shame through him, and he ran around the curve. There was nothing there, nothing but the trail along the ledge and the rock between him and the next curve. It looked like the trail widened out on the other side of the rock. Good. He would not mind a wider trail. Inside, he marveled at the white man and his horse. It would take much courage to be first on this thin rock ledge, both in man and in horse. It would be a horse worth having, and soon it would be his. He came up to the rock and stopped.

There was only a sliver of trail outside of the rock, and he could see scuff marks where the metal horseshoes had scraped the bare rock. It was amazing that the man could get his horse around that obstacle, but he obviously had. White Feather edged his way around the rock, back against the warm stone.

At first, when the ledge crumbled beneath his

Don Hepler

feet, he couldn't believe it was really happening. Automatically his hands scrabbled on the smooth rock for a handhold, but there was no handhold, and he felt himself begin to fall. The feeling of disbelief stayed with him. It was not possible. The white man and his horse had crossed in that very place. Then he knew. It had been a trap, a very clever trap, set by the white man. White Feather had been taken in like a small child. He twisted in midair in futile efforts to save himself, but his mind was remarkable calm, analyzing the trap, understanding the cleverness of the white man. He even felt shame at having been so easily taken in. He heard someone yelling, just in time to realize it was himself. He saw the women looking up at him open-mouthed, then watched the ground rush up and meet him.

"White Feather is dead," Two Dog told Yellow Knife. "He fell from the rock." Yellow Knife studied his brave.

"He fell?" he asked.

"He was being watched," Two Dog said. "He was alone when he fell." He hesitated. "He screamed like a small child," he added, "all the way to the ground." There was a note of contempt in his voice.

Yellow Knife thought about it. Another young man dead, another life on his shoulders. Stone Hand would be shaking his head in disgust.

He didn't think White Feather had simply fallen. There was no doubt in his mind that the man or men blocking the path had somehow been involved. Maybe it was some kind of trap or snare.

The white woman said something, looking right at him. Yellow Knife was annoyed. Women should not speak to a man when he was thinking. This woman would have to be shown her place. Then reason took over and he stayed his hand.

"What did she say?" he asked Light One.

"She says if she is set free her husband will kill no Indians."

Yellow Knife thought of White Feather and felt anger surge through him.

"He has already killed one of my young men," he said, harsh and hard. The woman stepped back from his tone, not understanding the words. Anger colored his vision. "He shall be killed and when he is dead, you will also be killed." Light One translated for the woman.

The woman paled but stood firm. After all, Stacy might be watching. She said something to Light One, speaking softly. Light One turned to Yellow Knife.

"She said that if her husband is dead she would rather be dead also." In spite of his anger, Yellow Knife was impressed. There was more to these whites than he had first suspected. They had courage. Those bluecoats had died fighting bravely; even the last man had been killed before there was peace. It was a good point to remember.

Marvin had worked his right hand free and was flexing his fingers, trying to work feeling back into them. The Indians were paying him no mind, their attention taken by the man on the cliff. When the Indian fell from the cliff, the women who had been walking around the captured men ran to the body where it lay twitching on the hard, sandy soil. Marvin took advantage of the time to loosen the rope from his neck. Several of the women had knives protruding from buckskin sheathes tucked into their belts in the small of their back, but Marvin knew which woman he wanted. He had been watching. The one with the dusky skin and the braided hair, the one with the white beads sewn into her garment, was Yellow Knife's woman. She was the only one who could save him and his sons.

He burst to his feet like a flushed grouse, running silently toward the gathered women. He burst through the crowd, knocking several roughly to the ground, and by the time the dust settled, he had Twisted Hair clasped to him, knife against her throat. There was a sudden silence among the Indians. Nobody moved. The white man on the cliff was suddenly forgotten.

Yellow Knife walked back to where the man

was holding his beloved Twisted Hair. How quickly things could change. First he was holding a white man's woman, threatening her with death, and suddenly a white man was holding his woman and threatening *her* with death. As the fear surged through him, he felt a sudden kinship with the man on the cliff. He walked up to where the two stood locked together, Twisted Hair's own knife held close to her throat.

"Tell him to release the woman and he can go free," Yellow Knife said to Light One. Light One spoke to the white who snarled back.

"He wants his sons set free also," he reported, "and the woman."

Yellow Knife thought on it for a moment, then said, "If he sets my woman free, they shall go free. But if he harms my woman, it will take many days for him to die, and then only after he has seen his sons die slowly." Yellow Knife was to be taken seriously. His mind was firm. He tried not to look into Twisted Hair's eyes. Light One put his words to the desperate white man, listened to a brief phrase, then turned back to his chief.

"He understands," he said. Yellow Knife nodded.

"Release the others and bring the white woman back here," he said. Several braves went to carry out his orders. In moments, Martha was there, looking at the scene. The expression on Twisted Hair's face caught her by the throat.

"Do not hurt her, Marvin," she said. "You are holding her too tight. The knife is cutting her throat."

"Shut up, woman," he snarled. "I am getting me and my sons out of here. You too, if you've a mind."

"Paw," called Johnny. "I reckon Fred's dead." Marvin's eyes turned smoky, first with hurt, then with anger.

"Damn you," he said to Yellow Knife, speaking hard and fast. "You killed my boy."

"Marvin, don't," Martha said. She could see the blind hate in his eyes.

"You boys mount up and ride out of here like the devil himself was after you!" he yelled. He was looking at Yellow Knife, face twisted in hate.

"Don't do it," Martha said. "Let's go with the boys. Let her go and let's go with the boys." She reached for his arm, but he jerked away and Twisted Hair gasped as the knife made another small slice on her neck.

"You reach for me again and you'll get to see the inside of her neck," Marvin hissed. Martha looked about frantically. She knew what was going to happen.

"Paw," called Johnny. "C'mon! We got the horses."

"I ain't comin'," Marvin yelled. "I got to stay with Fred. Besides, I can't trust these Indians."

"But Paw," from Johnny. "Fred's dead."

"I said git!" Marvin yelled. "When I say git, I mean git!"

"Okay, Paw," Johnnie said back. "We're leavin'."

"Have a good life," Marvin said. "Both of you. Know that Maw and I thought a lot o' the two of you."

"Paw!" Johnny called, distress evident in his voice.

"Git, I said!" from Marvin.

The soft voice of Light One trying to translate to Yellow Knife droned in the background.

The two horses thundered out of the camp.

"Marvin!" yelled Martha loud, distress plain in her voice. "Do not kill her!"

Marvin grinned an awful grin at Yellow Knife, who suddenly understood that Twisted Hair was about to die. He felt his inside twist in fear for her, in pain at his coming aloneness.

"Damn you for letting my boy die," Marvin said with soft, hate plain in his voice. "I'll see you in hell," Marvin added, and tensed himself to cut the woman's throat fast and deep.

"*Stacy!*" screamed Martha at almost the same instant as Marvin's head snapped back violently and the sound of a rifle shot echoed back and forth between the cliffs. A second shot was almost on top of the first, and Marvin's already dead body twitched as the heavy slug smashed into his chest, and then he was on the ground, motionless, broken head leaking red into the dust, not ten feet from White Feather's lifeless body. The echoes of the two fast shots rolled and rumbled away down the valley.

Yellow Knife found himself standing there, Twisted Hair wrapped in his arms. She was sobbing into his chest and he was amazed. He had never thought to see her cry. Her wracking sobs tore at his insides. He looked up; the white woman was watching him, expressionless. He suddenly realized this was not the action expected of a chief, and he stepped back from his wife, who stopped crying at once and stood there, straight and tall, ignoring the trickles of blood on her neck from the small knife wounds. Her breathing was jerky for a moment, then she had herself under iron control once more.

"I will finish cooking," she said.

"Good," he replied, then turned away from the woman he loved. Twisted Hair bent down and took her knife from the hand of the man who almost killed her, then walked back over to her fire.

Yellow Knife needed time to think, time to ponder on the happenings of the day, but there was no time.

"Shall I go after the two white men?" Two Dog asked.

"No," said Yellow Knife. "We still have their weapons. Let them go. Perhaps we shall capture them again someday and take more weapons from them." This didn't seem very likely to Two Dog, but he was impressed with his chief and would go along with his judgment. He saw several other young braves head out after the two white men anyway. Yellow Knife also saw them go but said nothing. It was what he would have done only last year when he was so much younger, when he had so much more freedom than he had as a chief. He wished them well.

The white woman was still looking at him, and she presented a totally different kind of problem. These whites were turning out to be nothing but trouble. She spoke to Light One.

"She says that if you let her go, her husband will kill no more Indians," Light One reported. Yellow Knife could hear traces of residual excitement in Light One's voice. It had been an interesting day so far for a man who was barely a warrior.

"Tell her to call her husband down," said Yellow Knife. "He will not be harmed." Light One translated the words. Yellow Knife watched a wry smile turn up the corners of the woman's mouth.

"She says she does not think her man will believe you," Light One reported.

"I do not want the advice of a woman," Yellow Knife said angrily. "Tell her to do as I say." Light One translated and the woman shrugged.

"Stacy!" she called. "Chief Yellow Knife says you should come down and they will not hurt you!" Everyone was looking up at the cliff, searching for the man with the rifle. A long minute passed. Yellow Knife spoke.

"Call him again," said Light One.

"Stacy," Martha called. "Chief Yellow Knife says you should come on down." There was no movement on the cliff.

Two Dog saw him first, walking down the center of the valley, stepping between the line of rocks, marching toward the gathered Indians. His rifle was in his left hand, and his right hand hovered casually around his Colt. Two Dog caught Yellow Knife's attention, and he too turned and watched the big white man stride toward him. One by one the Indians caught sight of Stacy walking toward them. It happened slowly, until finally the only person still looking at the cliff was Martha. She suddenly realized the others had all turned their attention elsewhere, and she turned to see her husband coming toward her, less than a hundred yards away. She broke into a run toward her man.

"Martha, stop!" he said, loud and hard. She stopped as if she had been shot, suddenly under control once more. She stood stock-still and drank in the sight of Stacy still walking toward the chief.

"I may need my hands free," he added by way of explanation, and she understood his order.

"I never thought you'd come down," she said without moving. "I didn't want you to come down." He shrugged.

"Seemed like the best time to me," he said. Just the sound of his strong, quiet voice made her feel better. Some of the tension went out of her chest. No matter what happened now, they would be together. She could hear the buzz of Light One translating to Yellow Knife.

Stacy stopped about twenty feet from the chief.

"Hello, again," he said. Light One translated. Yellow Knife nodded and studied the white man, Stacy. He was brave, for it would take courage to go down to the camp of an enemy. But now Yellow Knife no longer felt like an enemy. If this man, Stacy, had not shot when he did, Twisted Hair would be cold and dead on the ground, throat spread open in the afternoon sun. He spoke through Light One.

"Come," he said. "We will smoke and talk." A sudden relaxation spread through the camp, and the other Indians moved away to continue their preparations for the night.

Yellow Knife turned and led the way back to the seven rocks. He sat down on one and Stacy stood there for a moment, then sat on the one next to Yellow Knife. Martha stood off to the side, trying to think like an Indian, trying not to do anything to offend their captor, who was now their host. Not another word was spoken as they watched the tipis go up and the fires start. Children seemed to appear from nowhere, playing happily in the afternoon sun.

Twisted Hair finished with the tipi and fire, cooking a dog for their guests. She was trying not to look at the white man who had saved her life, but several times he caught her eye as she looked at him. Stacy could see the curiosity there, but she would look away immediately when their eyes crossed.

Some of the children grew bolder, coming over to stare solemnly at the white man and woman. Several even came over to Martha and touched her dress, feeling the cloth. In a moment their curiosity would be satisfied, and they would scamper back to their play. Martha was surprised at how these supposedly cruel people indulged their children. It was completely contrary to everything she had ever heard, yet the people smiled, laughed, and seemed happy and at ease in each other's company. Maybe they were not the savages they were supposed to be.

Chapter Nine

It was comfortable inside the tipi. The flaps were adjusted to channel the smoke outside, and the small fire provided enough heat and light to keep it friendly inside. The three men—Yellow Knife, Light One, and Stacy—sat silent around the fire until Twisted Hair brought the meat. The men ate first, then Twisted Hair motioned to Martha and they went outside and ate.

Martha wasn't certain what kind of meat she was eating, then decided she really did not want to know. Whatever it was, she was suddenly starved, and it filled her stomach and tasted sweet. The Sioux women watched her as she ate, offering more whenever she was ready. Once satisfied, she drank water from the creek to ''fill in the cracks,'' then sat back on her haunches like the other women and studied the camp.

As if by slow magic, there were thirty-six tipis where there had been none only hours before. It was as if a small town had been built in an hour. Children laughed and played and scampered around. She could hear the booming laughter of a man from somewhere in the camp and wondered what had just occurred to create such merriment.

There were people entering and leaving tipis, and smoke from the cooking fires and center of each tipi rose straight up until it reached the top of the cliff, where it was blown into shreds by the wind.

The whole impression was one of a friendly, happy community, a small town that moved with the people, but was as unchanging in its own way as the one where she had been raised.

The Sioux had not turned out to be anything like she had expected. There was none of the blatant cruelty she had anticipated. They were just people, not savage Indians, not a race of beings somewhat lesser than herself, as she had been taught. They were just people of a different color, with a different culture. They loved their children and laughed and loved just like all people everywhere. They got hungry and they slept and they hurt and bled.

She wondered what Stacy was doing, but

somehow she was not worried anymore. They could face anything together. They could handle anything together. They didn't have to worry about dealing with the Sioux, for she had learned something valuable. They were not unlike anybody else. She wished she could tell Stacy. Maybe he would figure it out for himself.

Having eaten, Yellow Knife carefully lit his pipe, then passed it across to Stacy. The big white man gingerly took the pipe, treating it with the respect it deserved. He carefully took a puff, then passed it back. His lungs sent a sharp and certain message that they did not care to have that smoke in them, but Stacy fought down the urge to cough. Somehow he didn't think the chief would find it funny.

Yellow Knife solemnly watched the clouds of smoke from the pipe waft upward, then exit the hole in the top of the tipi, bringing messages to his god. He was pleased that the white man had treated the ceremony with dignity.

"I am Yellow Knife, chief of these human beings," he said. Light One translated.

"I am Stacy Leech," he replied, "cattle rancher." Yellow Knife nodded.

"Two times now, you have shared my hospitality," he said. Stacy thought about that, then allowed a small smile to play at the corner of his lips.

"We are practically brothers," he said. Yellow Knife smiled slightly.

"You are guests in our camp and will be treated as welcome friends while you are here," he said. It was his intention to make their position and relationship pointedly plain.

"I had never doubted the word of Yellow Knife," Stacy replied matter-of-factly. Yellow Knife liked that answer.

"Your woman has said that we may stop and butcher some of your cattle each fall," Yellow Knife stated. "We can kill them and jerk the meat for winter."

"How many cattle?" Stacy asked. At the moment, the question did not seem very important because he figured he was likely to lose the ranch. If he had been able to make that beef delivery to the Army, a trust would have been established. They would have done more business, and maybe things would have been good. But life had never been real good to Stacy, and he could stand losing the land and the cattle and the security—as long as he got Martha back.

"Your woman said we could kill eight cattle," came the reply. A twinkle came into Yellow Knife's eye. "She bargained well for a prisoner," he added.

"My woman's word is my word," Stacy said back. Martha never ceased to surprise him. He was beginning to relax. "Buffalo are getting harder to find?" he asked.

Yellow Knife nodded. "Soon they will be gone, I think," he said. "I cannot imagine what the earth will be like without them. It will be hard for my people."

"Maybe you will raise cattle of your own," Stacy said.

"The Sioux are hunters and warriors," Yellow Knife responded, very serious. "I think that maybe when the buffalo are gone, the Sioux will be gone also."

"That is a sad thing to think on," Stacy replied.

"Even for a white man?" Yellow Knife wanted to know.

"I can only speak for me," Stacy said, "but I always figured the worth of a man by what he did, not what race he was."

"That was the reason for your war," Yellow Knife stated. Stacy nodded, impressed with the Indian's knowledge.

"Yup. Guess lots of others must feel pretty much the same way," he said.

"Then why do they not feel the same about the Indians?" asked Yellow Knife. Stacy frowned, not liking the question much. The silence dragged out. Only the muted sound of the fire and the subdued noise of the camp outside intruded on his thoughts.

"I think fear is the reason," he finally said. Light One's voice droned the translation for Yellow Knife. "So many white folk have been killed by Indians, killed in some of the worst ways we could ever imagine, that it just comes natural to think of all Indians as enemies." The silence stretched out once more as the meaning was taken from the words and pondered. "I think the Sioux and the Crow are enemies for pretty much the same reason," Stacy added.

Yellow Knife nodded as he thought on that. He was learning more about the people who were his enemies. He was also enjoying the conversation.

Twisted Hair came to Martha and motioned to her. Martha rose and followed the quiet Indian woman back through the tipi town to the other end. Here was where the body of Fred lay on the travois; there were several women around the body and they were doing something to it. Martha held back, not certain she wanted to see what was going on, but Twisted Hair indicated she should come forward. Reluctantly Martha stepped into the circle of women.

An old woman was hunched down beside Fred. She had a knife in her hand, and the blade had blood on it. In spite of herself, Martha looked down on the dead man. The woman had cut his arm, the one that was swollen big as a leg and blotched with the red stains of hemorrhaging under the skin that was a sign of serious snakebite. The cut was bleeding freely, and after a few minutes, the old woman pressed a pad of something that looked like brown moss against the cut to stop the flow of blood. Fred was bleeding! Fred was not dead, at least not yet.

Martha knelt down by his head and rested her hand on his brow. His skin was clammy, but not cold. His eyes fluttered open and he looked up at her.

"It's okay, Fred," she said, knowing that he could not hear her. She smiled, trying to comfort the hurt boy who looked up at her through the man's eyes. Fred looked almost satisfied, then his eyes drifted shut and he was unconscious once more.

Twisted Hair nudged Martha and offered her her knife. The implications were clear. Martha was free to kill the man who had been one of her captors.

Martha looked at the sharp blade, unable to imagine herself capable of sticking such an awful thing into anybody, no matter how mean and nasty that person was. She certainly couldn't see herself killing this man-child, a poor creature who could not hear or speak and had been trapped in his prison of flesh since birth. Far from hating Fred, she found herself feeling sorry for him. She shook her head.

Twisted Hair looked puzzled. Martha made signs that indicated Fred was deaf and could not speak. She pointed to her head and made the circle that was universally understood to mean a person was deranged, then pointed to Fred. She had no idea if she was communicating with Twisted Hair or not.

Comprehension dawned in Twisted Hair's eyes, and she said something to the other women, who rose and stepped away from Fred almost as if they were afraid contact with him would hurt them. Twisted Hair made a staying motion with her hand. Martha nodded and Twisted Hair hurried away into the village. Martha let her hand rest on Fred's forehead. Maybe he could tell there was someone who cared.

She felt a little awkward, kneeling there touching a man none of the others seemed to want to touch. The other women watched her in absolute silence, and Martha could hear the chirping of birds and the noise of children from the village. Idly she looked around, noticing that Marvin's body and the body of the Indian who fell were nowhere to be seen. She wondered what had happened to them.

Pretty soon she saw Chief Yellow Knife and Stacy coming toward her. Light One was trailing along behind. They stopped and looked down on her. Stacy's eyes took in the injured man, and his face was expressionless, but Martha could see anger in his eyes.

"This man has been touched by the spirit?" asked Yellow Knife.

"He cannot speak or hear," Martha replied. He is like a child in his mind." Light One translated. It had been the most interesting day of his life.

"Will he live?" Yellow Knife wanted to know.

"He is strong like a man," Martha explained. "I think if he is not dead by now, he will not die at all."

Yellow Knife nodded and spoke to Twisted Hair. She turned and in a moment several men appeared and started erecting a tipi over Fred and Martha as she knelt there. It took only a short time. Twisted Hair came in with a gourd of water that she laid by Fred's head, then she left, obviously glad to be going. Martha could hear the men talking outside, and in a moment Stacy came in.

It was the first time they had been alone in days, and Martha rose and reached out for the man she loved. Stacy held his wife, and for the first time in what seemed like a long time she felt safe, warm, and secure. Finally, she opened her eyes and looked up at him.

"I missed you," she said simply. Stacy nodded down at her, and she was stunned to see tears in his eyes, silent tears rolling down his cheeks. She had never imagined, not in her wildest dreams, that this man could cry, but he was crying. And he was crying over her. She snuggled her head back against his chest, warm all over, and they were content to stand like that for a long minute.

Fred stirred a little and they looked down at him.

"What's wrong with him?" Stacy asked.

"He's like a poor, dumb child," Martha said. "He never meant me any harm. He's just a child, trapped in a deaf-and-dumb man's body."

"Pretty big body," Stacy commented.

"I had noticed," Martha answered. They held each other for a while longer. "Are the Indians going to kill him?" she asked.

"I don't think so," said her husband. "Seems like they think he is some kind of big medicine who has been touched by the Great Spirit and all."

"Are they going to kill us?"

"Nope," he said. "They figure we are guests, entitled to all the hospitality they have to offer." There was another quiet spell.

"I'm glad you didn't let Marvin kill her," Martha said.

"Seems like it worked out for the best," Stacy commented.

Twisted Hair brought three buffalo robes into the tipi. She paid no attention to the two people holding on to each other in the center of the floor.

She kept a close eye on Fred, however, alert to any change in his condition, ready to flee if need be. When she left, there was no doubt she was glad to go. She closed the flap behind her.

Stacy and Martha looked at each other for a moment, then Martha began to arrange the robes on the floor. They were home for the night. Fred moved fitfully.

Outside, the sun went over the edge of the cliff and darkness fell rapidly. In a very short time, the village fell silent as the survivors of another day slept the sleep of the weary.

The one hundred and five cattle raised dust from the grassy land, leaving a wide trail of flattened grass and torn earth. Frank was bringing up the rear with Ritchie off to the other side. They had their hands full because the cattle were not used to being herded and wanted to wander off and graze. Likely the animals would not have time to get used to traveling, since the trip was to be so short.

Penny stepped in a hole and the jar shot a stab of pain through Wesley's head. He felt the bandage on his head. He was lucky to be alive, sure enough.

It had been his intention to take out after Stacy and Martha to wreak vengeance on the men who took her and tried to kill him, only there had been

rain and all tracks were gone. The guilt of responsibility weighed heavily on him. If not for
him and his secret troubles, nothing bad would
have happened to Martha.

When he found the sale contract for the Army,
it seemed that making good on the contract was
the only thing he could do to help make up for
the harm that was done on account of him. And
so he talked the boys into staying on, guaranteeing
them their rightful pay on his own.

The boys actually enjoyed rounding up the
cattle; the first hundred or so in a roundup were
always easy, although every one of Penny's foot-
falls had spiked pain through Wesley's head. Now
they were riding herd on the reluctant animals,
one hundred and five in all, stubborn and stupid
to the last one.

Lemuel would keep things going back on the
ranch until Stacy and Martha got back. The boys
would likely miss Lemuel's cooking something
awful for the next couple of weeks, but they'd
make out.

And that was the best that Wesley could see to
do; it was the only way he could help pay back
for all the trouble. He tried not to think about Martha too much or imagine what could be happening
to her. The awful guilt was just about too much
for a man to bear.

It was about three hours before sundown when

they put the herd to bed for the night in the large arroyo just outside of town. Five or six more days should see the fort come into sight, least if everything went even close to all right.

The four men came together at the opening of the arroyo.

"You boys cut out two beeves and take them in to the Railroad Cafe," Wesley said. "I'll stay with the herd." He could see Ritchie's face light up at the thought of seeing Alice again, and he smiled. "Keep Ritchie from doin' anything foolish," he added. Frank and William grinned at the boy, who looked kind of sheepish. "Eat some supper while you're there and tell Alice to take the price of the food off the price of the cattle. Tell her I'll be in to settle up and get supper soon as you boys get back to the herd."

"'Kay, Preacher," said Frank, and that was all there was to it. They never questioned his authority, just swung their horses and proceeded to do what he had told them to do. In no time, they were pushing two beeves toward town, and soon Wesley was alone with his horse and one hundred and three of the dumbest animals ever put on the earth. He sat on Penny, watching for any animal that might want to leave the arroyo, but for right now they seemed content to munch the long grass right where they were. His stomach rumbled dangerously.

Let's see. Take the boys a half hour to get to town, a half hour to drop off the beeves and get settled for supper. Near an hour to eat and let Ritchie play games with Alice, and fifteen minutes or so to get back. Best he could hope for would be about two and a half hours before they were back. He looked at his watch. Six o'clock. His stomach rumbled again. It sure would be nice if Alice stayed open till he got there, but nine o'clock was pretty late for her. He took a piece of jerky from his saddlebag and ripped off a bite. That should hold him.

Nine o'clock found him riding into town. A few lights were still on in some of the homes. The sheriff's office was lit up yet, and Wesley saw the square of yellow light as the door opened and the twisted form of Sheriff Borlan hobbled out to see who was coming into town at that late hour. Wes nodded at the man and pulled up in front of the cafe.

Alice opened the door and came out.

"Hello, Wesley," she said. She looked nice in her gingham dress and white apron, hair pulled back and pinned.

"Hello, Alice," he said as he swung down. She held the door for him and they went inside.

Wesley had no way of knowing that Alice had changed clothes and prettied herself up, but Sheriff Borlan had eaten in there that very night and he noticed right away, even from across the street. He allowed a smile to play across his lips before he went back into the office and closed the door behind him.

Chapter Ten

Wesley rode the left flank of the herd, keeping them pointed into the newly risen sun. He did the herding automatically, almost without any thought at all. His mind was on the previous night, and he was confused clear down to the center of his being.

Women were a complexity he would likely never understand. Alice had sure thrown him for a loop last night. He kept going over it again and again in his mind.

"You taking over for Stacy while he is gone?" she wanted to know.

"Not taking over," he said, "just helping out some."

"That's real nice," she came back.

"Most anybody would'a done it," he said, embarrassed by the topic. Besides, he wasn't helping out just to be nice; it was more like a penance, really.

"I saved you some supper," she said.

"Good. I am hungry enough that Penny was beginning to get nervous on the way in," he came back.

"Penny?"

"My horse."

"Oh," she said and laughed, a musical little laugh that he found quite appealing. In fact, he wished she would do it again.

It wasn't any time at all and she had brought out a steak with potatoes, beans, bread, and cool milk—for the both of them.

"Hope you don't mind if I eat with you," she said.

"Proud to have the company." And he thought no more about it.

They sat there and ate and talked about her life with her paw and the restaurant. Then they talked about his life out at the ranch, and the attack on him and the abduction of Martha. They talked about the beeves and how much she was to pay for them. And then, much to his surprise, supper was over. The fresh-baked apple pie was gone and the coffeepot was empty. It was late. He pulled out his watch, popped open the cover, and grunted in surprise.

"It's late," he said. "Ten-thirty already."

"You going to spend the night in town?" Alice asked.

"Nope. Got to get back to the herd."

"I see," she said, then rose to her feet and walked him to the door. They went outside into the night. He could hear the crickets all around town. Theirs was the only light in the whole town.

"I enjoyed talking with you, Wesley," Alice said as she looked over the dark town.

"Me too," he replied, surprised to realize it was the truth. It had been a long time since he had talked to a woman, really talked to her, and Alice was mighty easy to talk to. Like she understood what he was saying the first time, and like he could say things to her so easy that he didn't have to watch every word and ponder over whether they would be mistook.

They were standing there shoulder to shoulder, only she didn't hardly come up anywhere near his shoulder. They stood there for a minute like that, neither having anything to say. Finally, he put on his hat and turned to her.

"Well, I got to be going," he said, or at least tried to say. He only got out the "Well . . ." part, which sounded like "Welp . . ." actually, and suddenly she was putting her arms around him and reached her face up and kissed him full on the mouth.

Well, to say he was one surprised cowhand was to put the little on the way he felt. It was almost like he had been shot again, and his eyes opened wide and he wondered at the strangeness of her soft lips pressed on his. And then, to beat all, he discovered his arms were wrapped around her, and he was kissing back just as good as he was getting. She felt all warm and soft against him as they stood there front-to-front, and she felt almighty short too, what with him bending down to reach her and her straining up to reach him.

Then she pulled away and looked up at him, her eyes glinting in the reflected light from the lamps in the cafe.

"Oh, my," she said, and he didn't know how to take that then and he didn't know how to take it now.

She had practically run inside and closed the door and left him standing there like a fool with his arms still reached out as if they were waiting for her to come back, and an expression that must have been comical as all get out had anybody seen it.

He could hardly remember the ride back to the camp, but he could vaguely remember Frank nodding to him. The others were sound asleep already, and Wesley had turned in and gone to sleep still in a state of shock. He swore he could still feel her soft form pressed against him as he drifted to sleep.

The others had switched off the guard duty during the night, but did not wake him on account of they knew he had been out late tending to business . . . least they thought he had been tending to business.

His thoughts were brought back to the here and now when Ritchie rode up beside him.

"Hey, Preacher, you get to see Alice last night?" Ritchie wanted to know.

"Yup," Wesley answered.

"She say anything about me?" Ritchie asked. Wesley thought on it.

"Nope," he said finally. Ritchie looked disappointed.

"You sure she didn't say nothin'?" he asked again.

"Not a word," said Wesley. He wondered what Ritchie would say if he knew what had really happened last night.

"Dang!" Ritchie said, and spurred off after a wandering beef.

Wesley watched him go and sighed. Sometimes life was too complicated to bear thinking on. That was when he noticed the mounted Indian on the crest of the small hill ahead. For the moment, Alice was pushed back from the front of his mind. Life had just gotten a whole lot more complicated all of a sudden.

Not one to hold back when getting on forward

was indicated, he spurred Penny enough to get her moving out toward the Indian. He might as well find out what was going on. He slowed as he got closer and loosed the thong on his gun, walking Penny up to the waiting Indian. When he topped the hill, he could see the man's tribe stretched out in the valley below. There were more than a hundred of them.

He walked Penny up to the Indian. He pretended not to notice that the warrior was wearing an Army jacket and an Army holster. Where the Indian had got that stuff was something he didn't think he wanted to know, least not right now. The Indian held up his right hand in the universal gesture of peace.

"Hello, white man," the Indian said.

"Hello," Wesley said as he raised his own right hand. At least the brave could speak English.

"Many cow," the Indian observed, looking at the herd. Wesley said nothing. As the other Indians drew nearer, he could easily see the flash of blue jackets; the braves had Army rifles, breech loaders. He nodded.

"Many cow," he agreed.

"Trade for," the brave said bluntly.

Wesley's first impulse was to refuse. He didn't have any beeves to spare. Well, there *were* three extra, but he had brought those along as insurance against losing any on the trail. At the time he thought he was probably being overly cautious, but now it seemed like maybe a good idea.

"Trade what?" Wesley asked. He didn't like this situation at all, could see plenty of possibilities for trouble and only a couple of possibilities for peaceful coexistence. Trading seemed like a better and better idea all the time. He marveled at the quantity of Army clothing. Some Army unit must have had a bad time of it.

"Trade these," said the brave, and he held out a handful of coins, some gold, some silver. Wesley wondered where the Indian had come up with all the money, then remembered the uniforms and decided he didn't want to know.

"Trade three cow for three of those little gold ones," he said. The brave looked puzzled. Wesley kneed Penny over right next to the Indian and pointed to the gold twenty-dollar pieces.

"Fair trade?" the Indian wanted to know.

"Fair trade," Wesley said, and it was, too. The Indians would get three beeves, and he and his men would get to live, which seemed worth the three beeves all by itself. They could deliver the rest to the Army, and Stacy would get paid for three beeves that were actually expendable. The brave carefully took the three coins, the only three gold ones he had, and laid them in Wesley's hand. Wesley waved casually at the herd. Pick out the three you want, he was telling the Indian.

Three other braves rode up to the two men, and they all rode down to the herd together. Frank and the boys were riding at the front, waiting to see what was going to happen.

"Let them cut out three," Wesley said. "They already paid for them." Frank nodded, and the four white men rode at the front of the slow-moving herd as the Indians cut out the beeves they wanted and drove them back up the hill. All in all, it was a fair deal for all concerned.

It was a strange scene later when the Indians and the herd passed each other. The boys kept the herd moving and over to one side, while the Indians filed past going the other way. The two groups studied each other as they passed, curiosity showing in more than one face on either side. Some of the Indians were hurt bad, being pulled along behind the tribe on travois.

The Indians filed into the dust of the herd, and the herd plodded on over the tribe's trail. Then they were nothing but small dots on the horizon to each other, and finally they were gone. Frank rode up to Wesley.

"Okay if'n I start my heart beating again?" he asked.

Wesley grinned. "Don't ask me. I haven't breathed in the last hour myownself."

Frank laughed, then grew serious.

"Lots o' Army clothes on them braves," he observed. Wesley nodded.

"Seventh Cavalry they was," Frank continued. Wesley could think of nothing to say. Frank rode alongside in silence for a while, then wheeled and went back to his station at the rear of the herd.

Martha woke to the noise of movement outside, a lot of movement. Stacy was nowhere to be seen. She crawled over to Fred, almost afraid to look, afraid he was passed on and she had spent the night with a dead man. But he was not dead at all; in fact, he had better color and seemed to be sleeping. His arm still looked pretty gruesome, though. It looked like he was going to survive after all.

She leaned back on her haunches and studied him for a moment. What must it be like to do all that suffering, all those years of living, trapped inside a tomb of flesh. He must have the same feelings and wants as any other man, and doubt-less because he had the mind of a child he could not understand what he was feeling or what was happening to him.

Martha wondered what it would be like to go all those years being treated little better than a dumb animal by most of those around him except for his immediate family and without being able to communicate with another human being except for a few signs. How much suffering did God have in mind for this poor man-child, and why? What reason could there be to make anybody suffer like this poor creature must have suffered?

He would likely never be loved by a woman, would never laugh, would never be able to scream and rave against the pain in his mind. He would never be like everybody else.

His mother and father were dead, and likely his brothers were too. How could he get on all alone? She shivered. Never had she seen anyone so isolated. Even when he was surrounded by people, he was all alone inside.

"Best come on out," she heard Stacy say softly from outside. She brushed back a stray hair on Fred's tortured brow, then went outside to be with her husband.

The Indians were moving on. None came over to say good-bye, none even acknowledged the presence of the two white people standing by the tipi watching them slowly file away down the canyon. Martha and Stacy stood there side by side in silence and watched as the tribe disappeared around the bend in the canyon, and then they were all alone. Their horses were standing there tied to a small bush.

"I could'a used some breakfast before they left," Stacy observed.

Martha thought on that, and maybe it was the relief or the joy of being together again, or maybe it was just giddiness, but she found that remark extremely funny. She laughed. She laughed the delighted laugh of a little girl, tickled through and through. When she saw Stacy's expression as he looked down on her, she laughed all the harder, and soon tears of mirth were on her cheeks and then the laughter hiccupped and bubbled away and she was finally silent once more. She was next to her man. They were alive.

"You all done laughing at me, woman?" he asked, a twinkle in his eyes. She punched him lightly on the arm.

"Probably not," she said. He grinned at her.

"Probably be a good idea to get on out of here," he said.

"Probably."

He went over and untied the horses—all three of them.

"I knew you wouldn't leave him here," she said, thinking of Fred.

"Tell the truth, I'd like to shoot the . . ." Stacy said.

"No you wouldn't," Martha said back. "He's just like a little boy. You'd not be able to live with yourself if you shot him, or even if you left him behind to die all alone." She gave him an affectionate smile. "You may come across to others as hard and cold sometimes," she said, "but inside there's a whole lot more to you than most folks know."

Stacy paused from hooking up the travois. "Don't be too sure, woman," he said. She smiled. Let him think whatever he wants. She knew more about him than he did himself. She went over to help him get ready to go. They worked in silence, and in less than thirty minutes they were mounted and moving, Fred bouncing on the travois behind.

"You keep getting took by strange men," Stacy observed.

"Some stranger than others," she said. He raised an eyebrow and looked at her. She tried to look innocent.

"How come they took you?" he asked, ignoring her little-girl act.

"They believe that poor Mr. Hader killed their mother, Marvin's wife," she replied. "I do not have any of the gruesome details, but I cannot believe he was capable of such a thing." She paused. "I am sorry he is dead," she said. "I liked him; besides, I would love to ask him to explain what this was all about."

"He ain't dead," Stacy said. "Least he wasn't when I left."

"I saw them shoot him in the head!"

"Only creased him," Stacy explained. "Hit him pretty hard, but he wasn't dead."

"Good," she said. They rode in silence for a while.

"It will be good to get home," Martha said.

"Yeah," said Stacy. He wondered how much longer they could stay on the ranch. Once a man didn't follow through on an Army contract, his future was limited out here on the frontier. They could likely last another year or so. Maybe he could take up farming. He actually shook his head. Nope. No farming. He could not work the dirt. It wasn't inside him. He was a cattleman—or a gunfighter.

On the bluff, Buck lay on his stomach, watching the small procession beneath him. Why were they taking Fred's body with them? And what had happened to Paw?

Johnny was likely dead. Buck had been hiding in the small cutback when three young braves had passed, hot on the trail of his little brother. It was mostly certain they had caught up with him, although Buck had no proof of that.

So he had likely lost both Paw and his little brother. The only one he knew about for certain was down there on the travois, and according to what Johnny had said yesterday, Fred was dead. Now why would those two want to take a dead body along with them? Come to think on it, why would they want to take him along even if he wasn't dead? It was a mighty big mystery.

Buck eased back on the bluff and, once out of sight, mounted up. He would just follow along unobserved. Maybe something had come up, and besides, he wanted to know what they were going to do with Fred. Fred wasn't much of a brother, but dead or alive he was the only family Buck had left. He would tag along until they buried him. The sun beat down, and he wished the Indians hadn't taken his hat.

Buck's hat was resting comfortably on the head of Two Dog, Sioux warrior. It was another symbol of his prowess in battle, another indicator of victory over the white man. He felt even handsomer than before, even prouder. He could feel the eyes of every unmarried woman in the tribe, and even some of the married ones, as they watched him and wanted him. He rode straight and tall, trying to look bigger and stronger.

Yellow Knife watched Two Dog with some amusement. It was strange, but even though they were almost the same age, he looked on Two Dog as a father might look on a son. He felt so much older, so much wiser; he looked down on his child, on all his children, with the distance and height presented by maturity and wisdom. Yellow Knife was a chief. Stone Hand would be pleased.

Chapter Eleven

By the end of the second day, there was no doubt that Fred was going to survive. He was conscious now, his eyes wandering back and forth as he looked around. Tomorrow would likely see him well enough to sit a horse, and they could abandon that hated travois.

The sun was but a hand-width away from the horizon when Stacy made camp and set out to hunt some dinner. Hunting hadn't been too good, likely because of the large number of Indians who had been around. He didn't like to go too far away from the camp, either. It wasn't that he was worried about any trouble with Fred, but rather because of an uneasy feeling that had been nagging at him as they rode for the last two days.

146

Somebody was watching them. He never had any hard proof, but it just seemed as if eyes were peering down from the bluffs over on the left.

A small antelope hopped and frolicked across the grass just out of rifle range, and Stacy waited until the animal went out of sight behind a bush, then dismounted and began to stalk what he hoped would be supper.

Martha watched her husband grow smaller as he rode off. She always felt so alone when he was gone, so vulnerable. When he was around she felt safe and secure and assured. Funny how a man could do that just by being around.

Fred was sitting up on the skins from the travois. Since he regained consciousness, he spent a lot of time watching her. She could occasionally see the puzzlement on his face as he tried to piece together what had happened to his family; what had happened to the life he had known, the *only* life he had known. She could tell that the new unknown caused him no end of distress. She took the canteen over to him.

"Hello, Fred," she said, knowing full well he couldn't hear her. It made her feel better to talk to him, though. His eyes locked on hers, and she could see the depths of his confusion, the pain of his sudden bereavement, the severity of which he couldn't yet know. He gave her a tentative little smile.

She pulled the cork and handed him the water, which he took gratefully. He tilted it up and glug-glugged down what seemed like a quart before he lowered the canteen and handed it back. He had been extremely thirsty, and he had not been able to convey that to her in any way. She patted him on the head, then went back to her preparations for supper.

She tended the fire, putting on the pot with the very last of their coffee. The final chunks of Stacy's beef jerky went into a pot of water to boil. Even if he did manage to shoot something, the salt from the jerky would help flavor the meat.

And then, there he was, riding out of the grass, antelope slung over his saddle. The aloneness went away and the safeness returned. Martha smiled and stood, waiting to welcome her man.

Fred ate a tremendous amount of food, trying to replace all the life and energy the snakebite had sucked out of him. His eating habits were not pleasant to watch, but it was good to see him re-turning to life from where he had been.

"Look at him eat," she marveled. "Looks like he's going to make it all right." Stacy watched Fred for a while.

"Snake probably died," he said wryly. Martha made a face at him. They chewed on tender an-telope steaks for a moment.

"So what you planning on doing with him?" Stacy asked. It was a question that had been troubling Martha mightily, ever since she realized the big man-child was going to survive.

"I don't see how we could turn him out in the world on his own," she said carefully. Stacy's eye glinted as he looked at her across the fire. She dearly wished she could read his thoughts.

"You're thinkin' we ought to take him in," Stacy said flatly. It wasn't a question really, but it required an answer nevertheless. He knew it and she knew it.

Martha looked at her husband. She didn't know why this was so important to her. After all, the man-child had been part of the group who took her and tried to kill Mr. Hader. Had his paw told him to kill her, she had no doubt Fred would have done it without any feeling whatsoever. So why was it so important for her to show this man-child mercy and compassion?

Might be because of the awful life Fred had lived. Might be because she could see how he doted on her now, how he watched her every move, like a son might watch his mother. It was all too complicated to put into words. If only she could get Stacy to understand. She sighed. That might not be too easy. Likely Stacy would still like to put a bullet into Fred, for Stacy was not the type to show pity to anyone who hurt one of his own.

She looked over at Fred, who wiped his mouth on his sleeve and lay back on the skins, exhausted. He would be asleep in moments, she knew. It must be a nice way to sleep when there was no sound whatsoever to disturb a body. Fred's eyes glinted in the fading light as he gazed at her. She could see the adoration in there, but it not anything evil or nasty, just the wondrous love of a child for his protector, his mother almost.

"He's not much to look at," she said. "He's not much on manners, either, but he's a human being and I don't think he has ever been treated like one." Fred's eyes slid closed and he was gone, leaving her alone with her husband. She paused, waiting for Stacy to speak, to object maybe. He remained quiet. He had plenty of time now, time to let her form her thoughts and put them across to him. She looked at him, then looked away.

"One of our men killed his mother," she went on. "One of us killed his father. Most likely the Sioux killed his brothers. He doesn't have anyone but us." She gave another big sigh. Stacy's face stayed emotionless.

"I think I can make him into something worthwhile," she said. "I can help him be a better person, help him become someone of value instead of just a freak of nature." She looked up at Stacy. "Say something, man. Am I making any sense at all?"

"You think he loves you like a mother," Stacy said flatly. "You think of him as more child than man. You think you can make up for some of the emptiness in his life. That's about what I see here." He sipped at his coffee and frowned at the cup without being aware of it. The coffee was weak on account of the grounds were all gone and the flavor was just plain boiled out of what was left. He took another sip. At least it was hot.

Martha looked at her husband, a little surprised. This quiet man, this man of unpolished words, was more perceptive than she had thought. He had used his plain way of speaking to put his thoughts out precisely for her to see. They were good and true thoughts, teaching her more about the way she felt inside herself than she had known before.

"I guess that's it," she said. "You figured it out better than I did." She sat back and waited for his decision. An owl hooted off in the distance, and the fire smelled of mesquite.

"Well," he said, "I guess most everybody should have a pet."

Martha was taken aback. What did that mean? Then she saw the tiny twinkle in his eye.

"He is going to take a really big leash," Stacy observed, and in a second Martha was across the fire and in his arms.

"Oof!" he exclaimed as she knocked the wind out of him.

"He will learn to love you too," she said, "just like a father." Stacy grunted.

"Not if he finds out that I am the one who busted a cap on his real dad," he said. That took some of the joy out of her right away, and she laid there in his arms and thought that over. In a minute or two, her thoughts turned away from Fred, and she realized how comfortable she was. Stacy's arms were soft around her, and she felt safe and warm and finally at peace.

The unmistakable sound of a shell being jacked into a lever-action rifle snapped her eyes open and her head around. Buck stood there, Stacy's rifle leveled at the two of them. Stacy didn't move a muscle.

"Evening," Buck said and showed them his crooked teeth in a big grin.

Martha looked at him in amazement for a moment, then got mad all over.

"That does it!" she said, and got to her feet. "I've just about had it with people pointing guns at me and taking me wherever they want to take me." She held out her hand. "Now you give me that gun and you give it to me right now."

Buck's expression showed how shocked he was. Uncertainty played across his face as he looked at the fiery woman.

"C'mon," she said. "Give me that darned thing and do it right now. I am not going to ask you again."

For a moment, Stacy thought Buck was actually going to hand the rifle over to her. Buck lowered the long gun from his shoulder and started to reach it out to her, then suddenly seemed to realize what he was doing. He leveled the rifle on Stacy where he sat.

"Sit down, Martha," he said, hard and plain. "Sit down or I'll plug him where he sits."

Every fiber of her being wanted to go for him, wanted to get inside that rifle and tear at his face with her fingers. Martha was fed up with being threatened and mistreated, fed up with being scared. But his words forced clarity into her mind. If she did anything foolish, it wouldn't be her that would get shot, it would be Stacy. She had just gotten him back. She did not want to lose him again. She sat down.

"Now you stay down," Buck said, still hard. The rifle shook slightly in his hands with the force of his emotions. It was still aimed directly at Stacy.

"And you," he practically hissed at Stacy, "you killed my paw. I just heard you tell her. I aim to do the same for you."

"Buck, no!" Martha yelled. "You must've heard him say he was going to take care of your brother. If you kill him, you'll be hurting your brother."

"You can take care of my brother," Buck said,

eyes never leaving the face of the man he intended to kill.

"You kill my husband and I'll kill you!" Martha shot back, voice hard as his. "I'll kill you and I'll kill Fred too." Stacy looked at her, surprised at the vehemence in her words and tone. No doubt that woman thought highly of him.

"You'll be eating my cooking," she went on. "You'll have to sleep sometime when I'm around. You'll never know when it will come, but by God, it'll come."

Buck looked down at her, uncertainty on his face as he thought about her words. Her tone left no doubt she meant every word.

"Then I'll just have to kill you too," he finally said, the idea setting hard with him. "I won't like it none, but I guess that's the only way. I got to make up for him killing Paw." He almost sounded like he was trying to make her understand and approve. A movement from Fred caught their attention.

Fred rolled to one side, eyes bright. He struggled up to his knees and painfully began to crawl toward toward his brother. He held Buck with his eyes as he struggled against the obvious weakness and pain. His progress was slow, ever so slow, and he placed one knee down, then the next, ignoring any rocks in his path. His face was twisted with the strain of his effort, sweat beading and glistening on his forehead as they watched. Buck seemed fascinated by the sight, but the rifle never wavered from its point of aim.

Stacy wished he had not left the thong on his gun. At least if he had a chance, any chance, no matter how slim, it would be better than sitting there and silently waiting for that man to shoot him dead. He thought frantically, although his face never changed expression. There had to be something he could try, some way he could stop this man before he could kill him; some way he could tear the life from this man before he could kill Martha. My god! How could anybody even think of killing Martha!

He had the knife in his boot. It was the only weapon he could get out fast. He would go for the knife and try to get to the man. It was all he could do. No doubt he would be shot, but if he didn't die right away, maybe he could get his hands on that awful face with its crooked teeth. If he could just get close to him before death took him, it would be enough. He would kill that awful man, stab him with the long, razor-sharp blade. Most likely they would die together, but maybe, just maybe, Martha would make it okay. That was the only chance he could see to save her.

He wrote himself off as being already dead, and waited for Buck to give him the slightest opportunity, the split second of hesitation that would be all he needed. The rifle had to move. If it went off where it was pointed now, he would be dead. He would stand no chance at all, and neither would Martha. First the rifle had to move. Just an inch or so would do it—just so it wasn't pointed at the center of his head. He watched Fred crawl toward his brother. Maybe Fred would do something, take Buck's attention away for a second. Stacy waited.

The mere fact that Fred was moving with purpose was remarkable. His face was twisted with the effort, eyes scrunched almost completely closed. Painfully he crawled toward his brother. All three watched the extraordinary effort in silence, as if out of respect for the suffering Fred was putting himself through.

Finally Fred was there, on hands and knees in front of his brother. His head hung down and they could hear him panting with the strain of his effort. He wavered there, rocking from side to side, then collapsed in a pile on the ground in front of his brother. Martha wanted to go to him, to help him, but the rifle unwaveringly aimed at her husband's head kept her frozen in place.

Fred turned his head to the side, reached out with a huge, very pale hand, and took his brother by the foot. He looked up at Buck, and Buck looked down at him, but the rifle never moved.

Fred slowly shook his head. Don't do it. The message was plain to everyone there.

"Help him," Buck said to Martha. She did not move.

"No," she said. "You help him. Then ride away." They were all watching Fred as he continued to shake his head, eyes imploring his brother, *Don't do it. Don't do it, Buck.*

Then the poisoned body could take no more; the eyes slid closed and the head rested on one of his big arms. His chest rose and fell with his breathing. He was out cold again.

"I will help him and then I will ride away with him," Buck said softly. He's the only family I got left. I can take care of him good."

"No you can't," said Martha. "Think about it. You've lived with him all his life. Do you think you can really take care of him right?" Suddenly she knew what her husband was thinking, knew that he was seconds away from death. She looked at him and their eyes met. In that instant they told each other everything they had ever wanted to say. In that instant they both knew that love was the one single element that made their lives worth living. In that single instant, they said all that, and then their look changed and they both considered themselves to be dead.

Stacy flicked his eyes back to the rifle. Funny how large the hole in the barrel seemed when viewed from this angle. He wondered if he would see the slug, would hear the blast of noise. When he looked in Buck's eyes, he could see the resolve and knew that now was the time, the last chance, the final chapter in his life. He tensed himself to go, knowing that Martha was doing the same thing only inches away from him. A deep abiding sadness came over him. He would never hold her, speak to her, or look on her again. He jumped at Buck.

Chapter Twelve

A rifle crashed and the heavy slug took Buck just behind the left ear, turning him off like a switch. There was not the slightest reflex in him, not the slightest remnant of the life that had been his only a split second before. His head slammed over sideways onto his shoulder, and he collapsed like a vertical shaft of water into a puddle on the ground. Stacy had only made it up to a half-crouch when the shot blasted out, and he remained frozen there, trying to comprehend the sudden, dramatic turn of events.

A man rose to his feet behind some rocks and slowly walked toward them. There was something familiar about him, and in a moment Stacy recognized him. Wesley Hader walked up to them.

159

"Evening," he said, just like it was any other day. He glanced down at the crumpled body. "Hated to shoot him while he was holding a rifle on you like that," he said. "I was sort'a afraid he was going to pull the trigger when he went down. I waited long as I could."

"Think nothing of it," Stacy heard himself say. He was still a little surprised that he wasn't dead instead of Buck.

Wesley smiled at the understated reply.

"I am glad you are not dead, Mr. Hader," Martha said.

"Me too, ma'am," said Wesley. He grew serious. "I am surely sorry you got involved in my troubles, ma'am."

"Me too, Mr. Hader," she replied. "However, I should say you just made up for it." She looked at him quizzically. "Tell me, Mr. Hader, why were they after you? You didn't really kill their mother, did you?"

"Long story, ma'am," he said. "If you like, I'll tell you when we get back to the herd."

"The herd?" Stacy asked. "What herd?"

"Oh, I got a hundred head 'bout a mile back," Wesley said. "Takin' them to Fort Ellis like we were supposed to." He hesitated. "Figured it was what you'd want me to do."

"I don't understand," Martha said.

"I do," Stacy said. Wesley looked embarrassed and actually shuffled his toe in the dirt.

"Aww," he said. "Nothing special. If I take a man's money, I ride for him, that's all. Besides, those beeves aren't delivered yet. Lots'a Indians around too," he added.

"I had noticed," Stacy said dryly. He turned away. "I'll get the travois set up, and the four of us will be on our way."

"Who is that?" Wesley asked, nodding at Fred out cold on the ground.

"Long story," Martha said. "If you like, I'll tell you about it when we get back to the herd." Wesley recognized his own words coming back at him and he grinned.

"Fair enough, ma'am," he said. "Meantime, I'll plant this fellow right here."

Martha watched for a moment as Wesley went through Buck's pockets and, finding nothing of value, began to pile rocks on the body. Then she turned away and began to put out the fire. In a little while Buck's grave would be all alone, unmarked. Nobody would ever know he was there. It wasn't likely that anybody would care, either. Life was hard in the West.

Two hours later they were joined around another fire sipping on some of Frank's strong coffee and stuffing beans and bacon into their empty innards.

"It all leaves a bad taste in the mouth," Wesley said. He was looking into the fire as he prepared to tell his story, not wanting to raise his eyes, not wanting to tell at all, only he figured these people had a right to know. Stacy and Martha said nothing, just waited. Frank rose to his feet.

"Best be I check on the boys," he said, and he walked away. He swung up on a horse and rode out to the herd as they watched. Sometimes a man was meant to stay and listen, sometimes a man was meant to walk away and not know what was in the book. Frank had made his choice and Wesley was grateful. He cleared his throat and went on.

"The McFeys had a small place outside of Bliss, Kansas. Small ranchers. Ordinarily I would'a had nothing to do with them, only I got real sick, with the grippe—least that's what she called it, Mrs. McFey that was."

"Anyhow, I fell off my horse right in front of their place and when I woke up I was inside in a bed. A real bed. Couldn't hardly remember the last time I was in a real bed," he added, wonder in his voice.

"The Missus, never did find out her Christian name, was tending to me, putting cool cloths on my head and poultices on my chest and back. She kept stuffing soup down my neck, and it seemed like she never slept, only took care of me and kept her men fed. Her husband was not too proud about having me there, but she would hear none of it and kept on tending to me just like I was one of her own.'' He took a sip of coffee and glanced up at the two people whose attention was locked on him. He looked back into the fire, something he ordinarily would never do.

''I finally coughed up the worst of whatever it was and my fever broke,'' he went on. ''I was weak as a kitten, and just beginning to notice what was going on around me. First off, I noticed how the Missus was coughing and breathing hard. In less than a day, she was the one in the bed and I was sent away by her husband, Marvin. I barely had my horse saddled—no small chore for me weak as I was—when I heard the hollering from inside the house and I knew she was dead.'' He stopped again, remembering, thinking about how unfair life was and how it took the good and left the undeserving and bad. Stacy and Martha waited patiently.

''I sat there in front of the house on Penny, wantin' to go inside and feel bad with the others, only I felt so darned guilty. Hadn't been for takin' care of me, she likely wouldn't have passed on like that. Guess the husband felt pretty much the same way, on account of he came out of the house shooting. I beat it on out of there on Penny and pretty soon I saw they were after me. I finally gave them the slip in the rain and you pretty much know the rest.'' He sighed.

"It just doesn't seem fair that a whole family should come to a sorry end just on account of a good woman who took care of a sick stranger," he said into the fire. "A whole family dead and it is all on me to carry for the rest of my days. How do you make up for a whole family?" he asked without looking up. "How do you do that?"

They sat there in silence. There was no way to answer a question like that, no way at all. Finally Martha broke the silence.

"Not quite the whole family," she said. "There's always Fred." She indicated the still form with a nod of her head.

"Yeah," said Wesley. "There's always Fred." He paused a second. "What happened to him anyway?" he wanted to know. Martha's voice droned on as she told her tale of adventure.

Lots to talk about around the fire tonight. Off in the distance they could hear one of the cowhands singing in his awful voice to the herd and the stars became brighter overhead.

The next three days were relatively easy, a gentle pushing of the small herd with more than enough hands to do the job.

By the third day, Fred insisted on riding herd just like the others, and he proved to be remarkably adept at handling the sometimes reluctant animals. He still tired quickly, and his right arm was weak and blotched red under the skin, but his brute strength made up for some of that.

He would look around every now and then, and Martha knew he was looking for other members of his family, but of course he could not ask and as yet, they had not communicated the extent of his loss. That task would fall to Martha sooner or later, as soon as she thought he was healed enough to handle the strain. It was her intention to keep him and take care of him. The thought of him trying to make do on his own was too terrible to bear thinking on.

Three hours before sundown the fort came into sight, and by sundown the cattle had been corralled and the beeves signed over to the Army. It was then they found out about Custer and the massacre. It was a strange feeling to know they had all had contact with the same Indians who had perpetrated such an awful deed.

Come morning, they headed home with assurances from the Army that more business would come their way. Life was getting better.

The next day late in the afternoon, appearing like a malevolent spirit out of the blood-red sunset, Johnny McFey entered the fort. His clothes were torn and ragged, his boots worn out, but he was alive and many years older than when he had started this godforsaken trip almost a year ago.

When his father had started the search for the man he believed responsible for the death of his beloved wife, John still had family, two brothers and a father. Now he was certain he was alone in the world. Doubtless his father was dead, selling his life to those awful Indians so his sons could go free. He had seen Fred dead, motionless on the travois, and when Buck had split off in their head-long flight from the Indian camp, Johnny—no, it was John now, never to be a Johnny again—John had known he would never see his older brother again either.

Aloneness brought maturity, but at an awful price to be sure, and it was a silent, tight-lipped man who walked into the fort, the happy-go-lucky youth of less than a week previous gone forever. A sergeant studied him from inside the gate.

"Howdy, sir," said the sergeant. John looked at him through exhausted eyes, finally nodding in response.

"You look like you been through it, sir," the sergeant went on.

"Some," John admitted.

"Indians?"

"Sioux."

The sergeant appeared impressed. "You hear about Custer?" he asked.

John was bone tired; food, not gossip was the first thing on his mind, since he hadn't eaten since yesterday morning.

"Where can I get something to eat?" he asked.

"Reckon you do look a little peaked," said the sergeant. "No place to buy any food here, though. Maybe if the captain says it is okay we can have Cookie make you up something."

"Let's go see the captain then," said John. "I'm traveling with a lot of empty in me."

Captain Flinn had been dismayed at his assignment to command Fort Ellis. It was so far out of the way, it might as well be in another country, and the troops were not the highly disciplined lot he was accustomed to dealing with. Instead, they were a collection of the dregs of the Army, the castoffs from other outfits, men who were more trouble than they were worth.

But he was Army through and through, and if the Army thought he could do something valuable with the men and the fort, he would make it happen. But he had no idea what contribution he could make.

Indian trouble had not been a big surprise, but the massacre of Custer and his men had shocked the captain to the very center of his being. It was as if God had pointed out the way for him to be of value, and he would take his ragged troops, misfits to a man, and go out into the wilderness and smite the evil Indian in his own lair.

"You were a captive of the Indians?" the captain asked, surprised and just a little bit doubtful.

"Yup," said John.

"You were with Mr. and Mrs. Leech, maybe?"

John shook his head, he had already figured it would not be in his best interest to admit to being a woman stealer. "Don't know nobody called Leech," he said, voice weary.

"What can you tell us about the Indians?" the captain wanted to know.

"All I know," said John, "but it will likely be a much better tale if you can find your way clear to feed me first."

The captain studied him, weighing the value of the food against the value of the possible intelligence.

"Have Cookie fill him up," he said to the sergeant. "Then bring him back here."

"Yes, sir," the sergeant said, and he left with John in tow.

John sawed off another piece of beef and stuffed it in his mouth. The hollow feeling was finally going away. His plate was covered with beef and fried potatoes, and the cook kept his glass full of fresh milk.

"So you ain't heard about Custer, then?" asked the sergeant who was watching him eat. John shook his head.

"He and his men were massacred," said the sergeant. "Killed to the last man, less than two weeks ago. By the Sioux."

John stopped chewing, remembering the profusion of blue Army clothes on the Indians.

"I saw lots of Army clothes on those Indians," he said. "Army rifles too, and pistols and such."

"Captain'll want to hear that," said the sergeant. John nodded and went back to his eating.

"Sounds to me like you were with the same Indians that had Mrs. Leech as a prisoner," said the captain.

"That her name?" asked John. "Mrs. Leech?" Obviously, the captain had talked to the woman.

"What did you say your name was?" asked the captain.

"John," said John. "John Morgan."

"Thought you said McFey earlier," said the captain.

"Nope. I said Morgan," said John. "Always been a Morgan, always will be."

"So you were one of the men who took Mrs. Leech?" the captain asked casually. John shook his head.

"Nope. She was catched with four men, one of them sickly. Sioux already had me on account of they took me earlier in the day." It wouldn't do to let the captain know he was involved in a woman-taking, although it did somehow feel like he was betraying his family.

"Uh huh," said the captain. He didn't believe

this man, but short of chasing after the Leeches and bringing them back, there was no way to prove it either way. He could not spare any men to go after them, not if he wanted to put a contingent in the field, and he *wanted* to get out there and kill those Indians. Maybe he could trip this man up, though. Worth a try.

"The Leeches were here," the captain said. "Delivered a small herd, some of which you just finished eating. They left this morning with their hands." He leaned back and shook his head. "You know, one of their men is deaf and dumb. Not quite right in the head either." He carefully watched the eyes of the man before him, looking for any signs of increased interest. Nothing.

"Man had just survived a snakebite," he said, throwing out his last hook. No reaction. So much for trickery. It would probably be best if he pretended to believe this man, best to get him out of here and out of the way. He sighed.

"How many Indians were there?" he asked, continuing the interview.

In the morning, just after breakfast, Captain Flinn led forty men out of the fort.

They looked good, flags flying, horses snorting—just like a unit headed for fame and glory. They also looked just like Custer's force had, most likely, and the thought sobered the captain for a moment. Then his pride and professionalism took over.

They were mean and they were misfits, true enough. But they were *his* misfits, and they knew how to fight. Chief Yellow Knife was as good as dead, his hide hung over the captain's fireplace.

An hour later, John McFey walked out of the fort headed northeast. It was a long way to where he wanted to go. It would probably take him two weeks to walk it, but there was no other choice. He could and would survive out there, for he had something powerful driving him onward. Not being alone was a mighty draw for any man, and there was a brother out there. John McFey knew where.

Stacy and Martha sat on the porch watching the sunset. They could see their hands out in front of the bunkhouse pretty much doing the doing the same thing. Horses roamed around trying to find any grass that hadn't been chewed down to the ground, and several beeves were silhouetted by the setting sun as they stood motionless on top of the bluff.

"Pretty," Martha said.

"Yup," Stacy said and nodded. A long silence followed. A couple of crickets were warming up, screeching their night music over by the barn. Frank laughed at the bunkhouse.

"Fine supper," said Stacy after a while. Purple was beginning to creep across the valley as the red sky faded to a dull glow.

"Thank you, sir," Martha said, pleased. Feet on the railing, Stacy leaned back in his chair, teetering dangerously.

"This is about as good as it gets," he observed. They could see bats against the dying glow, flitting here and there catching insects.

They sat there in silence, watching as dusk turned into dark. Yellow light framed the bunkhouse door as the last man went in to bed. Stacy yawned.

"Guess it's time to turn in," he said.

"We're going to have a baby," Martha said. Just out of the blue. Just like that. There was silence from Stacy, then his chair teetered one time too many and he crashed flat on his back, sprawled like a big dummy on his own front porch.

Chapter Thirteen

Wesley found himself sitting on Penny in front of the Railroad Cafe. He sat there and looked at the place for quite a while, deciding whether to go inside, but he already knew he was going in; he had known it ever since he started riding this way earlier in the day.

He could see Alice tending her one table of customers, thought he saw her glance at him once from the corner of her eye, but he could be mistaken. Likely it was just wishful thinking on his part. The feel of her pressed against him front to front hung in his mind like a weight, coming down on him at the strangest times during the days since.

He swung down and went inside.

The other customers were the banker and his wife. It was said that she did not cook very well, and the two of them ate in the cafe pretty regularly just so her man could have a chance for his stomach to heal. They both nodded at Wesley, then turned back to their own conversation. She was a pretty woman, and Wesley allowed as how maybe cooking was not everything to a man, least not as long as he could afford to eat out every now and then.

"Hello, Wesley," It was Alice; she was standing there in her working dress, hair a little bit frazzled, flour puffs here and there on her apron. There were other stains on the apron, like cherry juice and grease. She looked beautiful.

"Evening, Alice," he said. She poured him some coffee.

"Heard you were back," she said. "Martha and Stacy too." The banker belched noisily. His lady rose, and his chair screeched in protest as he slid back and got up to go.

" 'Night, Alice," he said, and then they were alone. Alice poured herself a cup, set the coffeepot on the table, and sat down across from Wesley.

"Mind if I join you?" she asked.

"Proud to have you."

They sat there, engrossed in each other in the ways of new love. For him, nothing seemed to exist anymore except her. For her, there was innate surprise at his attention, at the fact that for once, life had given her exactly what she wanted the most. Neither of them noticed the man who walked up outside and looked in the window. He looked in at them for a long time, but he did not enter. In a few minutes, he walked away.

John McFey was tired and hungry. Seemed like he had been hungry ever since his last meal at the fort so many days ago. He'd left the fort with a purpose; to find his brother, and had the clothes on his back, his Colt with six rounds in it, and eighteen more rounds in his gunbelt. Now, fourteen days later, he was bone weary and had two rounds left in his Colt. That was all. He had spent the rest obtaining food, some days a rabbit, some days nothing. One glorious day he got two rabbits and almost had enough to eat for once.

Now he had but two rounds left, and a two-day walk yet to get to the ranch where his brother might be. Two more days. Two more rounds. He smiled grimly. Being hungry did make for improved shooting.

He walked into town just at dusk. Not that coming to town did anything for him, although it was nice to be in the vicinity of other people for a change. He had no money, nothing to trade.

He could smell food cooking before he ever reached town; his constant craving had somehow enhanced his sense of smell. Beef, that's what it was. Beef and coffee, and his mouth began to water. He could almost eat the smell he was so hungry.

He walked into town, not moving real fast anymore. It seemed that almost every muscle hurt—not the sharp hurt of injury, but rather the dull ache of abused and overused muscles, muscles asked much of but given little in return.

The cafe was the place that drew his attention, and in spite of his resolve to continue walking, his feet took him to the window where he could look inside.

First thing he saw was his reflection in the glass. His clothes were ragged and dusty, hat deformed and bedraggled looking. He had a scraggly beard and was amazed at how he could barely recognize himself. It was as if a dirty stranger looked back at him, the kind of man he would have once passed on the street with a snort of disgust.

He looked past the reflection at the couple seated at the table inside. They were sipping coffee, talking intently to each other. Sometimes they weren't talking, just looking. They were in love, he thought. The girl was pretty, and the man was Wesley, the man he had shot and killed so many days ago.

John stood there, shocked. Wesley wasn't dead. John had seen him fall, hit in the head with the rifle slug, but here he was. Tough sucker, that's for sure. He felt the weight of his gun on his hip. It was there. Two rounds left. All he had to do was shoot through the window and the man Paw had wanted dead so bad would be dead.

He thought about what the thirst for revenge had brought. Buck dead, Paw dead, Fred snakebit. Everything they had was gone, stolen by the Indians, and yet the man they set out to kill was still alive. Seemed like maybe if he was supposed to be dead, he would be dead. Maybe it just wasn't supposed to happen. Maybe the man was supposed to live for a while.

Not that John believed in God. Oh, he went to church with Paw and Maw on account of that's what they wanted him to do, but inside where he really lived and believed, he could not bring himself to believe in a god. Life was too hard, too nasty for a benevolent being to exist. He figured life had just proven him right too.

After all, Paw and Maw had both believed and now they were dead, killed without mercy even if there was a god—killed without mercy if there wasn't one either. Buck was dead, likely dying unpleasantly at the hands of the savages, and Buck had believed in God. He shook his head. Nope. Life was just too deep to think about sometimes. All a man could do was to live it best he knew how, and after all the scratching and struggling was finished, a peaceful dying was the best he could hope for.

John was surprised that he felt no anger, no animosity toward the man in the cafe. He was just a man, trying to get along as best he could. He had not wanted to make Maw sick, probably felt pretty bad about her dying too, especially after she had nursed him back to health like she had. Killing him would not bring Maw back, nor Paw nor Buck. Killing him seemed like it had cost his family everything they had to lose, and even had they succeeded, there would have been nothing to gain.

John took a deep breath, turned, and began walking west once more. Two more days. Maybe Fred was still alive.

Sheriff Borlan watched the man turn and walk out of town. Something had brought the sheriff outside. It hadn't been anything he could put his finger on, just a feeling that he should be outside and he had opened his door and soft-stepped outside.

The man was looking into the cafe, standing there motionless. He had been through some hard times, but he was wearing a gun and the sheriff had a feeling he was thinking about using it. Cyrus stood there watching, feeling the weight of the badge on his chest. He hoped he was wrong, hoped the man would not pull his weapon, for it was the sheriff's intention to fire on him if he did.

Cyrus had never fired on another living man and was not anxious to do so. But he would. That was his job the way he saw it, and if he had to shoot somebody to protect one of the citizens who hired him, he would.

But the man turned away and walked out of town, walking gingerly as if his feet hurt, and judging from the way he looked, they very well might. He must have come a far piece on foot, and that was a strange thing in this wide-open country. If Cyrus had been a bit more intelligent, he would have spent a lot of time wondering about that, but as it was he just watched the man walk out of town, then went back inside and closed the door.

Four hours later, John was lying under the overhanging branches of a scrawny old tree all twisted and deformed from its life of struggling against the winds and weather. He heard the horse coming long before it actually clopped steadily past. Had to be Wesley, and John stayed motionless as the man silhouetted himself against the moon for an instant and then clopped off toward the west.

The sounds of a summer night fell around him once more, and he lay there semiconscious as he thought about how nice it would be to have a horse again. And it would be nice to have some food too.

He wasn't exactly sure what he was going to

do when he found Fred—seemed like life was hard enough so each moment required his full attention—but likely he could get some food and then he and Fred could start back to see how much of their own land was still theirs. Old McBeavis had been licking his lips for that land for years, and once they up and left like they did, he likely began oozing his own stock onto their spread.

'Course the law was on their side, what with the land legally registered to them and all, but possession sometimes meant a lot, at least to the one who did the possessing at the time.

Sometime in the middle of that train of thought, sleep fell like a velvet blanket on the weary man.

John opened his eyes and looked into the small fire that crackled softly as it ate a few green sticks. Wesley sat across the fire, feeding it with ever-larger pieces until it was going good and proper. He looked across at John.

"Howdy," he said. Dawn was just turning the sky pink off to the east.

"Morning," John said back. Life was stranger and stranger all the time.

Wesley carefully sliced some bacon into a pan, and in moments the smell of cooking meat woke John's stomach. He could feel it roll and buck in anticipation. Wesley dumped a can of beans on top of the cooking bacon.

"Looked like you wouldn't mind sharing a fire," Wesley said casually.

"Didn't think you knew I was here," John said as he stretched life into his weary muscles. Lord, he hurt all over.

"Slept there myownself on occasion," was Wesley's comment as he stirred the greasy pan of food. John could not take his eyes off the golden beans and meaty bacon. Doubtless Wesley could easy hear his stomach kicking up such a fuss.

The bacon was barely cooked and the beans none too warm when Wesley spooned out a massive plateful and handed it across to John.

"Obliged," John said. He took the offered fork and dug in with gusto. The stuff was just over lukewarm, slimy with bacon grease, but it was doubtless the best food he had ever eaten in his entire life. Mouthful after mouthful was shoveled down as he watched Wesley put the coffee on to boil, and in what seemed like a short time, the plate was empty.

Without comment, Wesley filled it up again and handed it back across. He appeared to ignore the ravenous man, but he was watching him out of the corner of his eye as he tended the fire, waiting for the coffee to be finished. He recognized the man beneath the beard and the dirt.

The coffee was finally dark enough, and Wesley poured two cups and handed one across. He gingerly sipped at his own, trying not to burn his lips on the metal cup.

"You still figure on killing me, do you?" he asked casually. Across the fire the fork stopped in midair and the man looked at him steadily for a moment.

There was so much John wanted to say. He wanted to tell Wesley that it had been Paw who wanted the revenge, that the cost of vengeance had proven way too dear. He wanted to tell him that John had taken his try at killing Wesley and had got no pleasure from the thought that he had succeeded. Only he couldn't put all that to words.

"Nope," was what came out, then the fork continued to his lips.

Wesley studied the man for a few seconds. Seemed like he was telling the truth, sure enough.

"Fred is almost all healed up," he said, and once again the fork stopped in midswing.

"He's alive?"

"Yup," Wesley affirmed. The man's eyes flooded, and Wesley was embarrassed and surprised. This fellow took on another dimension. He wasn't just a potential threat, he was someone's brother. Family meant a lot to him same as it did to most everyone else.

"Likely Fred'll be glad to see you," Wesley suggested.

The man struggled with his emotions for a moment, then asked, voice a little shaky yet, "How's he making out?"

"He's helping out around the Circle L," Wesley said. "Seems content enough. Sure can eat more'n his share." The man smiled broadly.

"He always was a good eater," he said, almost to himself.

"You ain't done so bad yourownself," Wesley pointed out. The man grinned. "You finish up," Wesley went on, "and riding double we can prob'ly make it to the ranch in time for supper."

"You'll do that?" John was surprised.

"Way I see it," Wesley came back, "your maw, bless her heart, saved my miserable life. Least I can do is give her kin a hand if I can."

It took fifteen minutes to break camp, and then they were mounted and on the way. Penny wasn't too happy with carrying the extra weight, but she knew they were on the way home, and that quickened her step. They rode in silence for almost an hour.

"Listen," said Wesley, "What's your name anyway?"

"John," said John.

"Listen, John," said Wesley. "We get to the bunkhouse how 'bout you do *me* a favor."

"What?"

"Take a bath," Wesley said. John laughed and, carrying double, Penny plodded on toward home.